D1434469

PUFFIN BOOKS

The Puffin Book of
Horse and Pony Stories

K. M. Peyton was brought up in the London suburbs. Later her
family moved north and she studied at Manchester Art School,
where she met her husband, now a cartoonist. After a spell of
teaching and travelling abroad, they settled in Essex, where they
still live today, and had two daughters. Her passion in life is riding
her horses. Her husband sails, and together they go fell-walking.

She has written since she was a child and has had over forty novels
published, of which the best known and best loved must be the
Flambards quartet, which won the Carnegie Medal and the
Guardian Award.

The Puffin Book of Horse and Pony Stories

Chosen by
K. M. Peyton

Illustrations by
Neil Reed

PUFFIN BOOKS

PUFFIN BOOKS

Published by the Penguin Group
Penguin Books Ltd, 27 Wrights Lane, London W8 5TZ, England
Penguin Books USA Inc., 375 Hudson Street, New York, New York 10014, USA
Penguin Books Australia Ltd, Ringwood, Victoria, Australia
Penguin Books Canada Ltd, 10 Alcorn Avenue, Toronto, Ontario, Canada M4V 3B2
Penguin Books (NZ) Ltd, 182–190 Wairau Road, Auckland 10, New Zealand

Penguin Books Ltd, Registered Offices: Harmondsworth, Middlesex, England

First published by Viking 1993
Published in Puffin Books 1994
3 5 7 9 10 8 6 4

The Acknowledgements on pages 185–86 constitute an extension of this copyright page

Filmset in Set in 12/14^{1}/2 Lasercomp Bembo by
Datix International Limited, Bungay, Suffolk

Printed in England by Clays Ltd, St Ives plc

Contents

Preface   *1*

A Pony for Jean   JOANNA CANNAN *5*

Silver Snaffles   PRIMROSE CUMMING *19*

Rosina Copper   KITTY BARNE *51*

The Black Brigade   W. J. GORDON *65*

National Velvet   ENID BAGNOLD *73*

Jump for Joy   PAT SMYTHE *93*

Horse of Air   LUCY REES *107*

Another Pony for Jean   JOANNA CANNAN *121*

Who, Sir? Me, Sir?   K. M. PEYTON *139*

Smoky   WILL JAMES *157*

Acknowledgements   *185*

Preface

When I was a child I devoured pony books. There were a great many in those days, not so many now. This is odd, because I think there are as many horsey children now as there were then ... fashion, I suppose. (Yes, it happens in publishing too.) So putting together this anthology was a labour of love – it was harder to leave pieces out than put them in. My criterion was very personal: what I liked best. (This excepts my own piece, I hasten to add: one has no sentimental views about one's own writing.)

I was brought up in the London suburbs and my parents could not afford to give me riding lessons. I saved up all my pocket money and had one every school holiday, on Wimbledon Common. These lessons, and going to horse shows, were the high-lights of my life. For days afterwards I cried and cried, because I hadn't got a pony of my own.

Many years later, I thought of these times when I

rode my own racehorse out of the training yard to take him on exercise. Every stride he took I savoured, because I realized I had attained my heart's desire. I only owned a quarter of him and he never won, but that is not the point – the point is that I was where I had dreamed of being ever since I can remember, on the back of a beautiful chestnut thoroughbred riding over the Wiltshire Downs on a spring day. It had taken fifty years.

I didn't learn to ride until I was quite old. But, being so frustrated at not having my own pony, I channelled my feelings into notebooks and that was how I became a writer. And through being a writer I eventually earned enough money to buy my first pony. This was when I was thirty-five . . . I must be one of life's slow starters. It was a New Forest weanling, a poor little frightened chestnut foal. We called him Cracker and when he was old enough I broke him in (ha ha – he broke me in!) and my daughter rode him. He was a little devil. From that time on we have never been without ponies and horses, sometimes as many as five. People lent them to us and we bought ill-treated ones, or bargains, and not a single one ever turned out a dud. My daughter did all the riding and when she departed for college she left behind two high-powered animals, one a rearer, and one a bolter which I was too frightened to ride. I gave them away to good and understanding homes (where they both lived out the rest of their lives) and then decided to buy a horse for myself. I told my knowledgeable friend and she found me Essie, a six-year-old grey Irish cob, fourteen-and-a-half hands high, who was being sold from a show-jumping home because she could only jump four feet nine inches (one and a half metres). I thought that was plenty high enough for me but when she arrived I thought she was too hot. 'Persist,' said my knowledgeable friend – a good motto for life – and she was right: I learned, and Essie calmed down (not being asked to jump four feet nine inches every day), and became the light of my life.

She is now twenty-four and lives with her replacement, Buster, a fifteen-hand bay cob, and Pip, an even older grey mare who was once my daughter's eventer and whom I bought back later in her life to save her from going to a bad home. I still ride Essie, but mostly I ride Buster, who is a cocky, bucking beast but great fun. Of course, I only need one horse, but there is no question of parting with 'the old girls'. They have devoted riders from the village who come up to ride and groom them and talk to them, because they can't have ponies of their own . . . it gives me great pleasure.

K M. Peyton

A Pony for Jean

JOANNA CANNAN

The three *Pony for Jean* books were written in the 1930s, but their humour and freshness make them good for ever. I had *A Pony for Jean* on almost permanent loan from the library and knew it off by heart. The writer, Joanna Cannan, is the mother of Josephine, Diana and Christine Pulletin-Thomson who write pony books today.

I can't tell you about everything that happened to me at Hedgers Green, so I am going to tell you about the most interesting thing of all, and that was – riding.

I must explain first that we looked for a house near Hedgers Green because we had cousins who lived there, and those were the days when we thought the country was dull and Mummy said that it would be nice to know *someone*. I knew the cousins a little because when they were in London they used to come and have lunch with us, and they were all right as long as they were eating, but after lunch it used to be awful: they hardly ever spoke except to Shadow, and when they had finished speaking to him they used to stand at the window looking out and grumbling because there were no horses in London. There were two boys, Guy and Martin, and a girl called Camilla, who was a year younger than I was.

I should have been sorry for my poor country cousins if they hadn't seemed to despise me. They looked scornfully at my toys and said that my hut would hold twenty-four bantams or a dozen hens. Camilla never wore socks except in the depths of winter, and she asked me why I did, and I said because I was made to. Camilla said that once they had bought her a pair of socks and she had thrown them up on the stable roof and they had stuck on the weathercock. The gardener had got them down and then she had put them on the horns of the Ayrshire bull and nobody had dared to get them off again. Of course I had no stories like that to tell to Camilla.

I don't think the cousins were at all pleased about our coming to live near them. Mummy and I went to tea with them as soon as we had finished moving in and getting our small white cottage tidy. The children were all at home; it was almost the last day of the summer holidays. Their house was big, though it wasn't a baronial hall or an ancestral castle; and they had a huge garden and lots of field and a lovely wood where they had huts that they had made themselves. They were allowed to light fires there and cook things. But they weren't making fires that day. They were riding.

Cousin Agnes met us at the gate and she said, 'Come along. The children are in the paddock.' We went across the lawn to some white railings. On the other side of them was the paddock. Jumps had been put up there, hurdles with gorse stuck into them, and an imitation stile, and poles that you could make higher and higher. The cousins were jumping their ponies. They didn't stop when they saw us, but waved scornfully.

Cousin Agnes began to tell me about the ponies. She said that Guy's black one was a five-year-old that his father had given him on his last birthday. Its name was Blackbird. Martin's pony was called Red Knight. It was a roan cob, quite old but very clever. Camilla was riding a lovely little chestnut with a white star on its forehead. It was called after the evening star – Hesperus.

Hesperus was being very naughty. He wouldn't jump the stile and he bucked when Camilla tried to make him. Mummy said, 'Isn't he rather lively?' and Cousin Agnes said, 'Oh, Camilla's all right. She can ride anything.' I was looking at the ponies, the black and the roan and the chestnut flying along with the wind in their manes, and suddenly I wanted, more than I wanted puppies even, to hear someone say, 'Oh, Jean's all right. She can ride anything.'

Cousin Agnes said, 'I except you'd like to help unsaddle the ponies, Jean,' and she shouted to the cousins, 'Come along in now. It's tea-time.' Then she and Mummy went indoors and I stayed by the railings.

The boys went on jumping, but Camilla rode over to me. She said, 'What was Mummy saying?'

I said, 'She said you were to come in now. It's tea-time.'

Camilla said, 'Bother. It's always something.' She turned round and yelled at the boys, 'Tea-time!' Then she said to me, 'Do you like Hesperus? Would you like to try him?'

I said, 'I don't know.' I expect you will think that I was very silly and babyish, but you must remember that I had just seen Hesperus bucking.

'Well, do you or don't you?' said Camilla in despising tones.

Camilla is a year younger than I am and I felt furious, and Camilla's despising me seemed worse than anything Hesperus could possibly do. I said, 'Yes, I should like to try him,' and I started to get on.

Camilla said, 'That's the wrong side. And when you get on you should face the tail.'

I scrambled on and gathered the reins up anyhow.

Guy cantered up to me.

'I say, can you ride?' he shouted.

Of course I couldn't. I had only ridden ponies at the seaside where a boy ran beside you. But though Hesperus felt very bouncy under me and not at all like the seaside ponies, I was still so furious with Camilla that I shouted back, 'Yes, of course.'

Guy stopped his pony and sat there looking at me and grinning and suddenly I felt as if something had burst inside me. I was all rage right down to my toes and the tips of my fingers. I did the maddest thing. I pulled Hesperus round and rode towards one of the jumps at a canter.

I think Guy shouted at me, but I didn't take any notice. I rode towards the jump and it looked very high and suddenly Hesperus's mane and his little chestnut ears rose up in front of me, and the next thing I saw was the ground coming to meet me. There was an awful thump and I knew no more till I woke up on the sofa in the drawing-room.

I woke up rather slowly. The first thing I heard was Cousin Agnes scolding Guy. 'You're a perfect fool,' she said. 'You ought to have stopped her,' and she said to Mummy, 'Claire, I shall never forgive myself. I can't think why I've got such idiotic children.'

I said, 'It's wasn't his fault. He asked if I could ride and I said yes. It was my fault – really.'

Everyone turned round then and looked at me. I saw to my surprise that Camilla was crying.

Cousin Agnes said nothing, but she handed me a glass of water. I drank it and then I began to think what a fool I must look lying on the sofa like an old lady. Then I thought it didn't matter much what I looked like. For ever and for ever the cousins would despise me.

Mummy said, 'Well, it certainly was your fault if you said that, when you've only ridden seaside ponies. But perhaps it was worth it.' She quoted from poetry, '*One crowded hour of glorious life is worth an age without a name.*' I didn't know what it meant then, but afterwards at school it was explained to me, and I agreed with it, and I always write it when people with autograph books ask me to write in them.

Cousin Agnes said, 'Well, I daresay it's the right spirit, but it's made my knees knock and I could do with a cup of tea.' Once when Shadow had a dogfight with a Sealyham, my own knees had knocked, but it had never occurred to me that such a thing could happen to a grown-up. Somehow I think it was then that I began to like Cousin Agnes.

Mummy said, 'I should think that my idiot-child had better stop in here on the sofa.'

I knew that I had acted like an idiot, so I couldn't be offended, but I couldn't stay on the sofa any longer and be treated as if I was ill. I jumped up and said, 'I'm all right.' The room was whirling round me, but it stopped after a bit and no one knew.

We all went into the dining-room and I was only allowed a slice of thin bread and butter and a cup of tea. But there was a plate of cucumber sandwiches near me and I managed to get four.

Mummy and Cousin Agnes talked at tea and nobody else said anything. But when we had nearly finished, Guy said suddenly, 'If she wants to ride she might have The Toastrack.'

Cousin Agnes said, 'Oh, Guy, how can you?'

Camilla said, 'The Toastrack's mine.'

Guy said, 'He's not yours any more than he's mine or Martin's. You were only saying yesterday that you wouldn't be seen dead on him.'

Cousin Agnes said, 'Well, it's an idea. At least if Jean wants ever to ride again. Do you, Jean?'

I didn't know whether I did or not. My neck was beginning to ache and in my imagination I could still see the ground coming to meet me. But I remembered what had happened the last time I said, 'I don't know,' so I said, 'Yes,' with firmness.

'The Toastrack's awful,' said Martin. He had red hair and freckles and always said what came into his head without stopping to think whether it was polite or suitable. 'Daddy bought him out of kindness. He's been half starved and he's all over horse bites. He simply won't go. He can't jump either. We've tried him and he just crawls over leg by leg.'

'He sounds just the pony for Jean then,' said Mummy. 'But I'm afraid that just now . . .'

That is a polite way of saying that you have no money. But Cousin Agnes said hastily, 'My dear, if Jean would like him she can have him as a gift. Honestly he isn't worth anything. Your orchard would do him proud and you only need bring him in in the depths of winter. Nigel could easily spare you a load of straw occasionally and some hay. He would be all right for Jean to start on, but I'm afraid he's exactly as Martin describes him.'

'It's awfully good of you, Agnes,' said Mummy. 'What do you think, Jean?'

I thought that even if The Toastrack was awful and all over horse bites, he would be better than nothing; anyhow he would have a velvet nose and the smell of horses. What had happened was that in spite of being so stupid and pretending I could ride, and falling off and fainting and lying like an old lady on the drawing-room sofa, I had begun that afternoon to love horses, and once you've started you can't stop, and you would sooner look at the ugliest horse than at the loveliest pantomine, and you would sooner hear the sound of hoofs than the most beautiful music, and you would sooner smell the smell of stables than your mother's best scent.

I was eating one of my sneaked cucumber sandwiches. I swallowed it nearly whole and said, 'Oh, please let's have him.'

Cousin Agnes said, 'Oh, well, that will be very nice then, but I warn you he's no picture. Guy can bring him down tomorrow. Unless,' she said, for she was one of the few people who understand how awful it is to wait for anything exciting, 'you would like to take him home with you?'

'Oh yes, please,' I begged her.

She laughed and said, 'All right. If everybody's finished, we'll go and look at him.'

There was a terrific scraping of chairs and we all got up and went out into the garden and down the drive to the stables. Cousin Agnes said, 'He's out all night, but we bring him in in the middle of the day because the flies worry his sore places.' And as we got nearer to the stables, she added, 'Now prepare yourselves for a scarecrow.'

I went into the stable first. It was cool and dark after the sunny garden and it smelled lovely. I thought it was empty at first and then I saw that in one of the loose boxes there was a bay pony eating busily. He was frightfully thin. His hip bones stood out and he had two grooves running down his hindquarters, which I was told afterwards are called 'poverty marks'. He was a bay pony but his coat was all rusty and dusty and he looked a dull ugly brown, and his tail, which was black, was straggly and bald in places. I stood at the door looking at him and he turned his head round and looked at me. Now that I know his dear face so well and have groomed every hair on his body, it is difficult to remember him as he was then, but I shall never forget the long soft look he gave me.

The others came in, and Guy opened the door of the loose box. Most of us went into the loose box and the thick straw rustled. Guy said, 'I'll give you a leg up,' and I scrambled on The Toastrack's back. His backbone stuck out in a sharp ridge and was very uncomfortable to sit on.

Cousin Agnes told Mummy that he was over thirteen hands, and somewhere between seven and nine years old. She said, 'Really I feel ashamed of giving you such a dud. Jean must start on him and then we must see what we can do about a better pony.'

I suddenly felt that I didn't want a better pony. I was a dud too. I felt for The Toastrack.

Guy was awfully decent. He said, 'We've got an extra brush that you can have and a curry comb. Do you know how to groom a pony?'

I said, 'No,' humbly.

Guy went to get the brush and the curry comb, and Mummy and Cousin Agnes faded away to look at the garden. I don't know how they could, when they might have been looking at the dear Toastrack.

When Guy came back he was simply loaded. He had a saddle and a bridle and a halter as well as the brush and the curry comb. He put the saddle and bridle down and gave me the brush. He told me to lean all my weight on it when I was brushing, and he said that you got awfully hot.

Presently Mummy and Cousin Agnes came back and Mummy said that we must be going. Guy put on the saddle and Camilla put on the bridle and Mummy took the halter and the brush and comb.

This time I mounted on the right side and facing the tail.

The Toastrack walked very slowly down the drive and stood stock still at the gate while we were saying goodbye and thank you. When I tried to get him out into the road he wouldn't move, so Mummy led him. She said it was a funeral procession but I didn't mind. I could hardly believe that I was riding home on my own pony.

I said, 'I'm jolly well not going to call him The

Toastrack. How would Camilla like to be called Snub-nose or Martin Freckle-Face?'

Mummy said that it was certainly enough to give him an inferiority complex. In case you don't know, that means thinking you are stupider or uglier than other people, and it must be very uncomfortable. So as we went slowly along we tried to think of a beautiful name for him.

I thought of Sir Lancelot and Buccaneer and Bonny Dundee, but Mummy said that The Toastrack might get just as bad an inferiority complex from feeling that he couldn't live up to his name. She suggested countryfied names: Lad's Love and Sweet William and Harvester. Then we got silly and giggled and suggested names like Haystack and Midden and Mangle-Wurtzel and Corrugated Iron. You know how silly you can get if you once start giggling. I rolled about in the saddle and nearly fell off and Mummy's legs went weak and she leaned against The Toastrack and he stood still.

We decided not to be silly and we went firmly on. I still giggled at intervals. Then, as we were going through the village, we met some horrible boys. They pointed at The Toastrack and said that we were taking him to the knacker's and he would be made into sausages.

I was awfully angry with them. I didn't take any notice, but looked at The Toastrack's ears. He didn't take any notice either, but just walked slowly on. He reminded me of someone going to the scaffold and ignoring the rabble, and when he had passed the boys I said to Mummy, 'I know. Let's call him Cavalier.'

Mummy thought that that would do, so we decided. I have heard since that it is unlucky to change a horse's name, but I don't believe it, because I have never had any bad luck with my darling Cavalier. And his name must have been altered twice at least, because the cruel master, that he had before the cousins bought him out of kindness, didn't call him The Toastrack, but probably something dull like Jack or Tom.

When we got back to our cottage the sun was setting, and under the apple trees in the orchard it was shady and cool. We turned Cavalier out there and at once he started eating. We stood looking at him for ages and then I had to go in to supper and bed. But I could see him out of the bathroom window as I dried myself, eating happily under the round harvest moon.

Silver Snaffles

PRIMROSE CUMMING

In this story Jenny has no pony of her own but loves an old pony called Tattles who she visits every evening in his loose box. One evening Tattles says, 'Through the dark corner and the password is Silver Snaffles.' Jenny goes into the darkest corner of the stable and says, 'Silver Snaffles' and a whole magic world of ponies opens up to her. Every night she goes through the corner to ride and Tattles comes with her to introduce her to all his pony friends. She meets a boy, Peter, who visits in the same way. They ride together, in a beautiful country hemmed in all round by a lilac mist.

★

The Story of Pippin

'Tattles,' said Jenny when they got back, 'please do tell us what is on the other side of the mist?'

'And why the ponies are afraid to go through?' added Peter.

Tattles looked troubled.

'Everyone who comes here asks that sooner or later,' he said. 'And at one time we didn't so much mind telling them. But ever since the dreadful thing happened, it is almost too painful to talk about what is beyond the mist.'

'If we knew what it was all about, perhaps we could help you?' suggested Peter.

'You know, there might be something in that,' said Tattles. 'The trouble with us ponies is that we are nervous about things we don't quite understand. With someone to help us and encourage us we could do a lot more.'

'Tell them if you like,' said Jasper testily. 'Although I don't see what they can do to help.'

'I will,' said Tattles, spurred on by Jasper's tone. 'Those who would rather not hear, go and hide their heads in their mangers.'

Strangely enough, although Jasper and Barbary put on expressions of suffering, nobody took Tattles' advice. Instead several heads looked out of the line of boxes, among them Cock Robin's little broad, bay face. Tattles gave a snort and began.

'Beyond the mist live the People who have No Horse Sense.'

There was a dead silence.

'Is that all?' asked Peter at last.

'All! Isn't that enough?' exclaimed Jasper.

'No, that is not all,' said Tattles. 'There is the fate of Pippin.'

'Who is Pippin?' asked Jenny.

'Someone else tell them, I can't,' said Tattles.

'I will undertake the sorrowful task,' said Paul, waggling his grey head mournfully over the door of his box. 'Please listen carefully, for I am not going to repeat it. Pippin is, or was, a chestnut mare, and she lived at Number Four.'

Jenny's eyes immediately turned to the empty box with its pile of straw and unused saddle and bridle. The mystery was about to be explained.

'She was a charming pony,' went on Paul. 'Ex – er – exquisite head.' He glanced quickly at Jenny as he said 'exquisite' to see if she remembered how the word had once tripped him up. 'And a beautiful mouth.'

'Wonderfully clean legs,' chimed in Tattles, forgetting his resolve not to speak.

'Golden as the sun,' said Shannon sentimentally.

'Movements like a deer,' said Jasper.

'Temper and manners sweeter than the sweetest meadow hay,' said Cock Robin.

'I was under the impression that I was telling this story,' said Paul. 'You will understand from these remarks that Pippin was a lovely creature. She had been, in fact, a show-ring pony, and because of that she was just the slightest bit cocksure. Not conceited or vain or boastful,' he added rapidly, as the others looked ready to contradict, 'but just a little over sure of her own powers.

'And one day she made up her mind to explore beyond the lilac mist. She went. Nothing we said could stop her, although she thanked us for our advice. She walked out of her box with her usual gay step that we knew so well, and she has never come back to it since.'

'You mean, she never came back through the mist?' asked Jenny.

'Exactly,' replied Paul.

'Then we must go and look for her,' said Peter. 'Jenny and I will go if two of you will take us.'

'Impos –' began Jasper, but a new voice cut across his:

'I will.'

They all turned and stared at the speaker, whose head was looking over the door of a box some way down the line. It was a big black head with rather long ears and a thick, fierce-looking mane which stood up on end.

'I'm tired of all this jibbing and baulkiness,' he went on defiantly. 'I will carry Jenny if someone will take Peter.'

'Not me!' said Jasper promptly.

'I shall be very busy during the next few days,' said Barbary primly.

'My name is Dragon,' said the black pony. 'With a name like this a fellow should be able to go anywhere. If no one else will come, then Jenny and I will go alone.'

'I think it is very brave of you, Dragon,' said Tattles. 'It is a disgrace that we have not done more about Pippin. If I come too —'

'You can't, Tattles,' interrupted the other ponies. 'We can't let you go.'

'Somebody must take me,' said Peter. 'Jenny and Dragon can't go alone, but four of us will win through.'

No one spoke for a little while, but the stable was full of small, uneasy noises, shifting of hoofs, rustling of straw, gusty breathing.

'I will come,' said a very small voice at last. It was Cock Robin who had spoken.

'That's a good pony,' said Dragon. 'You're worth your weight in oats. Then we can start off whenever Jenny and Peter think best.'

'I can come the evening after next,' said Jenny.

'So can I,' said Peter. 'And that settles it.'

Jenny was afraid during the next two days that something might happen to prevent her from going through the Dark Corner. But everything went smoothly, and she met Peter again in the sunny stable. The first thing Tattles did was to present them with two long-shaped bags, tightly stuffed with something soft.

'Put these behind your saddles,' he said. 'They hold

oats and chaff. There may be no proper food for
ponies in the place where you are going. There's nothing like a feed to keep your spirits up; and if you ever
find Pippin she may want some too.' His voice broke
at the mention of Pippin.

Cock Robin was nervy and cross.

'Is my brow-band straight?' he kept asking.

When he had been assured by several people that it
was perfectly straight, he started to worry about the
girths of the saddle. Peter pulled them up several
holes, then Cock Robin declared that they were too
tight and pinched him, so they were let down again.

'When we've walked a little way and the saddle
has settled down on my back, you must be sure to
pull those girths up two holes,' insisted Cock Robin.
'If the saddle slips round and you fall, you'll find the
ground very hard in the place where we are going.'

'Let's start,' said Dragon, coming out of his box.

Jenny saw that he was much bigger than the other
ponies and very powerfully built. He seemed covered
with rolls and mounds of muscle. The other ponies
gathered round to watch them start off.

'We will keep your mangers full of food and the
straw in your boxes turned and aired in case you
should ever come back,' said Paul solemnly.

'My dear Paul, don't be so gloomy,' said Dragon. 'We
are going straight there to find Pippin, and then straight
home again, long before the bedding is in need of airing.'

'We shall probably be back for the next meal,' said
Cock Robin, cheering up.

'Goodbye and good going,' said Tattles.

Amid a chorus of 'Goodbyes' the four adventurers set out, all rather silent and thinking of what lay ahead. At the edge of the mist Dragon said to Cock Robin and Peter:

'Keep very close to me. Whatever else happens we must not get separated.'

So Cock Robin crept close to Dragon's big body like a brown chicken beside a black hen, and they went into the mist. It closed round them in lilac foids, at first smelling sweetly of dewy flowers. In spite of their nearness, Jenny could only see Peter and Cock Robin in outline, and even Dragon's head and ears looked far away through the mist.

'Don't try to guide us. Let the reins go loose,' said Dragon. 'In a place like this it is better to let your ponies choose the way.'

The two ponies trod cautiously forward, their outstretched heads and necks swinging from side to side as they picked their way. Jenny noticed that slowly the mist was changing colour from lilac to pearly grey, and from grey to a dirty, smoky brown. At the same time the scent of flowers and fields was giving place to a nasty smell in which the fumes of petrol, oil and rubber were strongest.

The mist began to get thinner, and Dragon, whose head was in advance of the others, said in a low voice:

'We are nearly through.'

Peter and Jenny gripped their saddles with their

knees. Another minute, and they would enter the Land of the People who had No Horse Sense.

The Land Beyond the Mist

Clip, clap, clop! From softly thudding on the turf, the hoof beats of the ponies changed suddenly and rang out on a hard surface.

'Roads!' said Dragon.

At the same time the mist cleared right away in front of them. The smell of oil and petrol became stronger, and mingled with gritty dust, and their ears were deafened by the roaring and popping of many engines.

They were standing on the edge of a broad, shining road which ran on either side of them. Up and down it roared and raced streams of cars and motor cycles, hooting on their horns or back-firing with loud, banging noises like guns going off. Although they were in such a hurry, the motors did not seem to be going anywhere in particular. After Jenny and Peter and the ponies had watched for only a short time, they noticed that many of the cars were driving aimlessly backwards and forwards as if just for the fun of seeing how fast they could go.

Every now and then one stopped and turned, and the rest of the traffic immediately piled up round it. But no one ever seemed to get very hurt, and they all straightened out and rushed on again.

A long red racing car swept by so closely that the wind of its passing blew up the ponies' manes. Cock Robin shied and nearly fell over the high stone kerb at the edge of the road.

'What a dreadful, dreadful place!' he cried. 'Whatever made me, a sane, sensible pony, think of coming here?'

'To look for Pippin,' reminded Dragon.

'Of course,' said Cock Robin, quietening down and looking determined. 'Although I can't see how one pony all alone could possibly live long in a place like this.'

'Well, we must make a good search before we think of going back,' said Dragon. 'Something is keeping poor little Pippin here against her will. She wouldn't stay here of her own accord.'

Their ears were becoming accustomed to the noise, so that they could talk together fairly freely.

'Where shall we start to look?' asked Jenny, staring rather helplessly at the shining road and rushing traffic.

As Cock Robin had said, it did not seem likely that one small chestnut pony could live long in such surroundings.

'Let's turn to the left,' suggested Peter. 'Left always seems to be the most important side with ponies. These people can't live in their cars. They must have houses and gardens somewhere. If we go far enough we are bound to come to some, and Pippin is more likely to be there than wandering about the road.'

'There is open country on either side of this road,' said Cock Robin. 'Don't you think she would take to the fields?'

But a high, iron fence with a spiky top bounded each side of the road, except where they had come through the mist, and there was no gate or gap where a pony could have got through or over.

'I think Peter's idea is best,' said Dragon. 'We had better go in single file along the very edge of the road.'

They started, Dragon and Jenny leading because Dragon was the bigger. The traffic was most confusing, for instead of keeping to one side of the road, it darted up and down and in and out without any rules at all. Dragon strode purposefully forward, but little Robin became so confused that when a car came unbearably close, he swung out into the road to avoid it.

Then he and Peter found themselves in the thick of the cars. He dodged and twisted and tried to get back to Dragon. His hoofs slipped on the oily surface and he came down on his side, throwing Peter clear. The traffic stopped, the leading cars so close that both Cock Robin and Peter found themselves looking up at rubber tyres and steaming radiators. The drivers and their passengers scrambled out, crying to each other:

'An accident! Come on, an accident!'

In a few seconds the spaces between the cars were so packed with people that there was no chance of Peter and Cock Robin getting away. More and more cars drew up on all sides, and more and more people came crowding round, telling each other in thrilled tones:

'There's been an accident! Shove up a bit, we must see!'

'Oh, my poor Cock Robin!' cried Dragon. 'I must get to him. If anything happens to him as well as Pippin it will break Tattles' heart.'

He thrust his broad chest and shoulders into the crowd, and snorted down people's necks in a most dragon-like manner, so that they let him pass. Cock Robin and Peter had got to their feet and seemed to have escaped injury. What troubled them most was the crowd, which pressed round them more closely every minute.

'If I can't get some clean air, I shall choke,' said Cock Robin.

'Do let us get away,' implored Peter. 'We aren't hurt.'

But the people would not let them go yet; they were enjoying themselves far too much, staring with bulging eyes and talking about 'The accident'.

'Dragon,' whispered Jenny in his ear, 'don't you think it would be a good chance to ask somebody about Pippin? Someone in this crowd might know about her.'

'Yes, but you ask,' said Dragon. 'They don't understand pony language here.'

Jenny selected the kindest-looking person near her, although none of them looked exactly unkind, only excitable and rather stupid.

'Please, have you seen a chestnut pony lately?' she asked a man.

He gaped up at her.

'A pony carved out of chestnut? No, of course not!'

'I don't mean a wooden pony,' said Jenny. 'I mean an ordinary flesh-and-blood pony with a lovely golden-brown coat and a tail and mane to match.'

'Oh, I see,' said the man. 'You better ask Mrs Jostlepot. *She'll* tell you about a pony.'

He pointed out a plump lady wearing a great quantity of flying scarves, trailing necklaces, jangling bangles and fluttering frills, and an enormous hat bristling with hat pins.

Jenny repeated her question to Mrs Jostlepot. The crowd began to lose interest in the accident and all gathered round to hear what Jenny had to say. As, in the meantime, even more cars were being held up, it looked as if the jam never would be sorted out again.

'Oh, my dear,' said Mrs Jostlepot, 'of course we have a pony. We are the only people to have one. Of course, there are a great many others would like to copy us, but luckily there aren't any more ponies to be had. Of course, we always have considered ourselves above our neighbours, and now that our children have a pony we –'

'But what kind of pony is it?' broke in Peter impatiently.

'My dear, I couldn't possibly tell you that,' said Mrs Jostlepot. 'My husband paid an enormous sum for it; but we are willing to pay anything in order to make a better show than our friends. I see that you have ponies too, which means that you must have the same tastes as we; that is the only reason why I am talking to you now.'

'But the pony,' persisted Jenny, 'what colour is it?'

'Oh well, I don't really know,' said Mrs Jostlepot. 'A sort of brown, I think, but I wouldn't be sure. The most important thing is that our children have a pony and our neighbours haven't. The little dears can look down on their friends now. As you take the same interest in ponies as we do, perhaps you would like to come along and see ours?'

'It must be Pippin,' said Dragon. 'She says it's the only pony in the place.'

'Yes, we'd like to come very much,' said Jenny. 'Is it far?'

'Only just along the road. I'll show you the way in the car,' said Mrs Jostlepot.

She climbed into her car, and the other people followed her example and got into theirs. Evidently Mrs Jostlepot occupied a high position among the People who have No Horse Sense. A man came up and caught Peter's arm.

'Would you sell me your ponies?' he asked. 'If my children had *two* ponies we should be able to look down on the Jostlepots.'

'They don't belong to us,' said Peter.

'And we shouldn't sell them if they did,' added Jenny.

The man seemed very disappointed. He went away muttering, but Jenny noticed that he kept looking back at them in a sinister fashion.

'I don't like that man,' she said to Peter.

Peter said that he had not noticed the man's looks. He was much more intent on watching Mrs Jostlepot get her perfectly enormous car out of the jam. She did it by the simple method of driving straight ahead and knocking all the smaller cars out of the way.

'Keep close behind me,' she called, flapping a large white hand out of the window.

This was not so very easy to do, for she roared away at nearly fifty miles an hour, leaving behind her a cloud of dirty blue smoke from the exhaust which nearly blinded them.

'We must keep up with her somehow,' said Cock Robin, starting forward.

Luckily, they had the road to themselves, for the cars Mrs Jostlepot had knocked over had to be set right again before the other people could move off. Far down the road ahead of them shot Mrs Jostlepot's car. Then they heard a shriek of brakes as it stopped, turned sharply and disappeared.

'I think that must be where she lives,' said Jenny.

They hurried along the slippery road as quickly as they dared. As they went they saw large pieces of paper blowing all over the place. Dragon and Cock Robin were nervous of these, and when a piece wrapped itself round one of Dragon's legs, even that brave person started, slipped and nearly fell down.

'No pony can stand white, blowy things,' said Cock Robin. 'And what a horrible lot there are!'

Besides the paper thrown down on the road, other bits were blowing about high in the air. There were also worn-out coats and old sacks thrown over the railings by the careless inhabitants, and these gave the ponies as many starts as the paper. All four were glad when they reached the spot where the car had disappeared, and found a drive leading up to a house. Mrs Jostlepot came to meet them.

'I was afraid you weren't coming,' she cried. 'I simply crawled along because I know ponies are so slow.'

She tried to stroke the ponies' faces with hands in white woolly gloves. Both Dragon and Cock Robin flinched away.

'If there's a thing I can't abide, it's being stroked with woolly gloves!' exclaimed Cock Robin.

Mrs Jostlepot did not understand pony language.

'What silly things, they won't let me stroke them!' she said, and promptly smacked their heads hard. Before Jenny or Peter could say anything, she went on: 'Come and see dear Figit and Funkie riding.'

She led the way round the side of the ugly house, painted in stripes of yellow and puce, and showed them a lawn in the middle of which stood a pear tree. Tied to the tree by a long piece of rope on her bridle was a little chestnut mare.

'Pippin!' said both Dragon and Cock Robin.

Mrs Jostlepot signalled to them to keep still.

'Just watch how well Figit and Funkie ride,' she whispered. 'Funkie is the handsome little boy on the pony, and Figit is the little girl with the lovely hair.'

Jenny and Peter and the two ponies watched in astonishment what was happening on the lawn. A little boy with a very white, fat face was astride Pippin. He held the reins so tightly bunched in one hand that her mouth was pulled open; with the other hand he held on to the front of the saddle, and even then did not look very safe or happy.

Meanwhile, Pippin was jogging round and round the pear tree on the end of the rope, which wound up shorter and shorter with each circle. When the rope was all wound round the tree so that she could go no farther, she turned round and began to unwind again.

Such a good idea, don't you think?' asked Mrs Jostlepot. 'There's no chance of the pony running away with the children. They are only allowed off the rope when someone is about. So safe, don't you think?'

As she spoke the rope got slack, and Pippin, putting a weary leg over it, fell down. She got up again quickly, and they were surprised to see that Funkie had held on to the saddle so tightly that he had been unable to fall off. Only his face looked a trifle more unhappy, if that were possible. Mrs Jostlepot did not seem at all worried by the way Pippin fell over the rope, and merely repeated:

'Such a safe idea!'

Then at last, Pippin, who had been toiling round with her head down, looked up and saw the little party.

'Cock Robin and Dragon!' she neighed. 'At last!'

Dinner with the Jostlepots

Dragon and Cock Robin could stay still no longer. They hurried up to Pippin with little, joyful nickers. When Funkie saw them coming, he thought they were after his blood. With a loud yell, he tumbled out of the saddle and went into hiding behind the pear tree.

'Have you come to take me home?' asked Pippin, with a world of longing in her voice.

'Yes, with the help of these two kind people, Jenny and Peter,' said Dragon.

'And me,' added Cock Robin, who hated to be overlooked, even in times of stress.

'Well, what do you think of our pony?' asked Mrs Jostlepot, who did not understand the talk going on between the ponies.

Jenny looked more closely at Pippin. She was thin and her coat looked dull and unkempt, and from time to time she gave a hard, dry cough, but it was still obvious that she was a little beauty.

'Are you sure that the saddle and bridle fit her?' Jenny asked.

'Oh, they must do,' said Mrs Jostlepot airily. 'You see, a long time ago a relation of ours kept a big hunter, and that saddle and bridle fitted it, so of course they will fit a small pony.'

The saddle nearly covered Pippin from back to tail, and her head and mouth were weighed down with a heavy double bridle and two great rusty bits. But Mrs Jostlepot refused to believe that what would fit a hunter would not do for a pony.

'You haven't seen Figit ride yet,' she said. 'Jump on, Figit dear, and show them how clever you are.'

Figit was a bony little girl with a sharp, peevish face and frizzed-out yellow hair.

'I'm sick of riding in circles,' she said crossly. 'Just as you are going fast it's time to stop and unwind again. Can't I go for a ride with them?'

'Why, yes, dear!' exclaimed her mother. 'That would be excellent. Our neighbours would then see what distinguished friends we have.'

Jenny and Peter did not want much to take Figit for a ride, but Dragon said:

'Do let's go. It will be a good chance to arrange how we are going to get Pippin home. It's lucky that Figit won't be able to understand us.'

Pippin was released from the rope and Figit scrambled on from the wrong side, because it was too much bother to go round to the left. She carried a hunting crop without a thong, and started off by giving Pippin a hard smack with it. Pippin seemed used to this treatment, for instead of plunging, as most ponies would have done, she merely broke into a fast trot.

'Goodbye, Figit,' called Mrs Jostlepot after her. 'Have a nice ride, and if you meet any of your friends, be sure and turn your nose up as you pass, because you have a pony and they haven't.'

Figit seemed to have one idea about riding, and that was to go as fast as possible. Whenever Pippin showed signs of slowing down, smack went the crop and she started on again. Dragon and Cock Robin were forced to keep up the same pace because they were anxious not to lose sight of Pippin.

Bang, bang, bang! went their poor hoofs on the roadway, and the tendons of their legs quivered and jarred with each step. Now and then their hoofs slipped on the greasy surface, and Jenny's heart jumped uncomfortably each time this happened. Pippin slipped the worst of any, for her shoes were worn smooth and as thin as paper.

They turned down another road, where it was no longer slippery, but instead strewn with loose, sharp flints. Jenny and Peter were going to dismount and lead the ponies over, but Figit suddenly thought that she would like to canter.

Smack went the crop harder than ever, and gallant little Pippin started to canter over the dangerous surface. Figit rolled about all over the big saddle. Her arms flapped, her knees stuck out so that daylight showed between them and Pippin's sides. She held all four reins in one hand and her crop in the other, which she waved about in the air; now and then she shouted loudly for no particular reason.

Pippin soon stumbled on the loose flints, but she cleverly saved herself from coming right down on her knees. Figit, however, having no grip on the saddle at all, flopped off on to the road.

'Did you see me being thrown off?' she asked Jenny proudly. 'Wasn't I brave not to cry?'

Jenny wanted to say, 'No, I think you are a horrid, stupid girl.' But she did not, because they wanted to keep Figit in a good temper. So she just said:

'Yes, I saw.'

'Shall we all walk now? We've been longing to talk to you,' said Peter cleverly.

This pleased Figit. She let Pippin walk, and began chattering away to Peter, saying that she thought ponies were really silly things, and that she only rode because none of her friends could afford it. She hardly spoke to Jenny at all. Jenny was glad of this because she could listen to what the ponies were saying.

'We must get you away from here as soon as possible,' Dragon told Pippin. 'It is quite plain that if you stay with these people much longer you will be a wreck.'

'Yes. All this fast going on hard roads makes my legs swell up,' said Pippin. 'And the dust and petrol fumes are affecting my lungs: you've heard how I cough. And you would be horrified if you could see the places where this saddle has rubbed my back, and the bruises the bits have made in my mouth.'

'Poor Pippin!' exclaimed Dragon. 'It won't be for much longer. I think we could get you away while the Jostlepots are having dinner.'

'There's one thing troubling me,' said Cock Robin, who had been pondering over matters. 'Won't it be stealing to take Pippin like that? Mrs Jostlepot said that her husband paid a lot of money for Pippin.'

'That is a huge big fib,' put in Pippin quickly. 'They didn't pay a farthing for me. They met me wandering about after I had come through the mist, and I let them take me home because I thought they would give me some food, and they've held on to me ever since. They tell people that they paid a lot for me because it sounds grand. That's the only reason why the children ride me, to impress their friends. I believe that they would be secretly glad if I went. Funkie is scared stiff all the time he is riding, and Figit gets bored because I cannot go so fast as a car.'

'Then that settles it,' said Cock Robin. 'While the Jostlepots are having dinner, Jenny and Peter must get us all away.'

'Have you had enough to eat, Pippin?' asked Dragon.

'Yes, but such strange things for a pony,' answered Pippin. 'Whole loaves of bread, chicken food and dog biscuits. It gives me indigestion.'

'Don't forget the food Tattles made us bring,' Jenny reminded them. 'Pippin must have a good feed of proper food to get her strength up before we start.'

'Oh, good Tattles!' said Pippin. 'As kind and thoughtful as ever.'

Figit was enjoying herself talking to Peter.

'You must come in to dinner,' she said. 'We have better things to eat than anybody else.'

Just as they were getting back to the Jostlepots' house, they met two children walking with the man who had offered to buy Dragon and Cock Robin. Evidently they were friends of Figit's, for they said 'Hullo!'

Figit remembered her mother's instructions. She turned her nose in the air without replying, and made Pippin walk so close to them that they tumbled in the ditch.

'Those were the Robbingems,' she laughed. 'I bet they must be jealous of me!'

When they got in, Pippin was tied up to the pear tree again without Figit troubling to take off the uncomfortable saddle and bridle.

'Tie up your ponies too, and come in to dinner,' Mrs Jostlepot called to Jenny and Peter.

Figit led Peter in at once, and Jenny managed to stay behind long enough to give the ponies Tattles' food supply. She gave Pippin a whole bag to herself, while Dragon and Cock Robin agreed to share the other bag.

The inside of the Jostlepots' house was crammed with expensive and unwieldy furniture. The chairs they sat on were very cold and slippery, and the backs had carved knobs which stuck into their shoulder blades. The table was so laden with rich food that the smell almost took away Jenny's appetite, although as a rule she had plenty of room for good things.

The Jostlepots ate huge quantities of everything at amazing speed, and managed to talk hard at the same time. It was not surprising that none of them looked very healthy.

Half-way through dinner, Peter stood up and said:

'Do you mind if Jenny and I go and look at the ponies?'

'Certainly not,' said Mrs Jostlepot with her mouth full. 'Only be quick, there is a lot more food to come yet.'

Jenny and Peter hurried out, thinking that their plan was succeeding well. A great shock awaited them. When they reached the lawn, it was to find only Pippin standing by the pear tree. Both Cock Robin and Dragon were missing.

'Come quickly!' neighed Pippin shrilly. 'The Robbingems have stolen Dragon and Cock Robin for their children. I can't do anything until you untie me.'

The Race to Safety

Peter and Jenny could hardly believe their eyes and ears. For this to happen just when everything had been going so well seemed too terrible.

'Don't stand gaping!' shrilled Pippin. 'The more time wasted, the less are our chances of all of us escaping. Come and take off this saddle and bridle so that I can move freely.'

Peter ungirthed the saddle whilst Jenny struggled with the many puzzling buckles on the bridle, most of which had been done up wrongly. Fear that the Jostlepots might come out before they got Pippin away made their fumbling fingers clumsy. At last Pippin was free and trotted off in front of them like a golden-brown butterfly who had just broken out of an ugly, leathery chrysalis.

'This way,' she cried. 'Tell me if I go too fast.'

Peter sprinted after her easily, but Jenny's legs began to tire.

'Jump on my back,' said Pippin. 'We mustn't leave you behind, you are too helpful.'

For a moment Jenny wondered how she could mount without a saddle. Then Peter made his hand into a stirrup and gave her a 'leg up'. Jenny gripped Pippin's warm back and did not disdain to hold on by her mane. They must not waste a moment through her falling off.

'Keep your toes turned up as much as you can, that will help to keep you on,' said Pippin.

It was jerky trotting bareback, but Jenny stuck on grimly. She found that it really did help to keep her toes up. At last Pippin stopped before a high paling.

'The Robbingems live on the other side,' she said. 'You go through that gate.'

Peter opened the gate a crack and peeped through. Jenny slipped off Pippin and peeped too. On the other side was a house with a concrete yard before it. In the yard were Dragon and Cock Robin with the two children in the saddles. They were being led round the yard by Mr and Mrs Robbingem. Both children were weeping aloud with fear, but Mr Robbingem only smiled and said:

'Never mind, dears. We are better off than the Jostlepots now.'

'We must take them along past the Jostlepots' house, so that they can see us,' said Mrs Robbingem.

'I don't know what to do now,' whispered Pippin. 'If I come any nearer they may hear my hoofs.'

'Why, we will just go in and accuse them of stealing our ponies,' said Peter fiercely.

'I don't think that will do any good,' said Pippin. 'They won't give them up.'

'But horse-stealing is against the law,' pointed out Jenny.

'There aren't any laws in this place,' explained Pippin. 'People go on just as badly as they like. Because they have no Horse Sense they think dishonesty pays. Really they are worse off, because they can't trust each other for a moment. No, the only thing to do is to get Dragon and Cock Robin away by stealth, and then make a dash for it through the mist.'

There did not seem to be much chance of getting the ponies away at that moment. However, it was a good thing that the Robbingem children were now screaming so loudly that their parents were quite unable to hear anything else. If Dragon and Cock Robin had bucked and plunged, they could probably have thrown off their riders and broken away. But they were too kind-hearted to toss the children off on to the concrete, where they might be badly hurt.

'We must think of something,' fumed Peter.

'And quickly too,' added Jenny, looking back up the road to see if the Jostlepots had started out to hunt for Pippin.

It was Jenny's sharp eye which noticed the Robbingems' motor standing just outside its garage on the side of the house. From where the Robbingems were with the two ponies the car could not be seen.

'Peter,' breathed Jenny, 'if only one of us could start the engine of the car going so that the Robbingems would hear it. Then they'd think that somebody was stealing it and would rush off and leave the ponies. When that happened the other one of us could run in and get the ponies away.'

'I can start the car!' cried Peter excitedly. 'I know how engines go, though I'm not supposed to. If you dump off the Robbingem children on to the ground, Dragon and Cock Robin can run out of the yard, and we will all meet here again. Of course they will chase us and we must be ready to take to our heels.'

'What about me? What shall I do?' asked Pippin.

'You must keep watch here,' said Jenny. 'If you see the Jostlepots coming, neigh loudly and at once. We don't want to be trapped between the two families.'

'Is there another entrance to the garage, farther round?' asked Peter.

'Yes, a little way along this paling,' said Pippin. 'You can get to the garage without being seen.'

'Be ready to go for the ponies directly you see the Robbingems run,' warned Peter. 'I expect the kids will be only too glad to get off. You'd better mount Dragon directly you get there.'

Peter ran along beside the paling, then vanished. Jenny waited with thumping heart to do her bit, whilst Pippin kept a sharp look-out up the road. Luckily the car-drivers were much too busy seeing how fast they could go to notice the girl and the chestnut pony standing beside the paling. Jenny did not hear Peter start the car, but the Robbingems did. She saw Mr Robbingem give a start. Then he shouted to his wife:

'The car! Somebody's making off with the car!'

Letting go of Dragon's bridle, he ran wildly across the yard. His wife followed screaming, and forgetting all about her charge over Cock Robin. The two ponies hesitated in doubt, and in a second Jenny was through the door and beside them.

The two children were so frightened that they could not even scream now. They were soft, floppy little creatures, and when Jenny lifted them out of the saddles they collapsed in heaps on the ground and stared up at her with great, googling eyes.

'Where are Pippin and Peter?' was Dragon's first question.

'Pippin is keeping watch outside and Peter is joining us,' cried Jenny, mounting. Luckily the Robbingems had not had the sense to shorten the stirrups for their children. 'Let Peter get on you as quickly as possible, Cock Robin, or they will catch him.'

At that moment Pippin's piercing neigh sounded above the roar of the traffic.

'The Jostlepots are coming!' cried Jenny. 'Hurry for all you're worth!'

The ponies scuttled through the gateway. Jenny banged her knee against the post, but she was too excited to feel any pain. They met Peter just outside. He vaulted into Cock Robin's saddle at the same moment as the Robbingems burst out into the road in pursuit. Bearing down the road from the opposite direction came the Jostlepots' huge car, with sticks and umbrellas waving angrily from every window.

'Follow me, now,' cried Pippin, darting ahead down the road. 'I know my way about here better than you do. I've planned this escape for weeks.'

They brushed past the Robbingems, who, seeing that they could do nothing on foot, dashed back for their car. In a minute the three ponies and two riders were being chased by two car-loads of people. Other cars, seeing an exciting hunt taking place, swung round and joined in. This was more lucky for the fugitives than otherwise, for the cars that turned to help forced the cars already chasing to slow down and even pushed some into the ditch.

'We can't keep this up much longer on the hard road,' jerked out Dragon, pounding along. 'We've had such a lot of road work already.'

Pippin, however, knew what she was about. Suddenly she turned into the side of the road. There was a gate in the iron railings and it was open. Oh, the relief of being on the turf once more, even though it was lumpy, dried-up turf, fretted with ruts and sprinkled with molehills!

The ponies broke into a slow, careful canter to relieve their legs from the jarring trotting on the road. Before them was a hedge, beyond that another strip of turf and then the mist.

'Once there, and we are safe,' said Cock Robin.

'It won't be the same place as we came through,' pointed out Jenny.

'That doesn't matter,' replied Pippin, 'so long as we get through somewhere. They won't follow us farther than the mist, because they can't see to drive their silly cars. They will drive them almost anywhere else. Look, they are coming through the gate!'

Peter and Jenny turned in their saddles and saw that the cars had swung in through the gate and were bumping and chugging over the field. Now that there was more room, the Jostlepots' powerful car began to shoot ahead.

'They can't follow us if we jump this hedge,' said Peter.

'We shall have to jump big, because there is a stream on the other side,' Pippin warned them. 'You lead, Dragon, you are the strongest.'

Jenny and Dragon collected themselves for the jump. As Dragon surged forward, to Jenny on his back he felt strong enough to jump anything. Then at the last second he stopped dead, nearly sliding into the jump. Jenny could hardly believe that the bold pony had refused. She was about to tussle with him as she had done with Jasper, when he said:

'There are two strands of barbed wire through that hedge, and another strand on the other side of the stream. Nobody with any Horse Sense would try to jump it.'

'Turn left, then,' cried Pippin. 'There's a gate and a bridge.'

She galloped alongside the hedge, and they followed at full stretch, for the cars were bearing down on them. This gate was open too.

'It's lucky for us that these people always forget to shut their gates behind them,' panted Pippin. 'But this bridge is not at all safe. You riders had better jump off and go over on foot.'

The bridge was made up of a few rotten-looking planks with brushwood thrown on top. Pippin darted over and a plank snapped beneath one of her nimble hoofs. Peter and Jenny jumped off, although it was awful to have to dismount when the chase was getting so hot.

'Cock Robin first, because he is the lightest,' commanded Dragon.

Peter and Cock Robin scrambled over, leaving another hole in the bridge. Jenny grew white. She felt sure that although she could get over safely, it would never bear the weight of Dragon. But the Jostlepots' car was nearly on them, and there was no time in which to stand doubting.

She ran across with the rein in her hand and Dragon

followed. There was the crashing of twigs and planks, and the splashings as they fell into the stream below. Then Dragon did a desperate leap which carried him half-way on to the bank. His hind hoofs broke right through the bridge, but with a kick and a mighty scramble he saved himself and heaved up into the field.

Hard upon their heels followed another crash. The mad Mrs Jostlepot had tried to drive over the bridge. It gave way right beneath the car, which was now wedged in the stream, where it would take a long time to get out again, and successfully blocked the way for everyone else.

The three ponies cantered unhurriedly over the turf, Jenny and Peter chuckling aloud with glee. They plunged into the dirty fog, holding their breath to keep out the smells. Then, when it gave place to the cool, lilac haze, they took great gulps of the sweet air, arriving through in a field not very far from the stables.

'I hope you have kept our straw well aired,' remarked Cock Robin cheekily, as they entered the stables.

'And a bite of oats wouldn't come amiss,' said Dragon, putting on an air of unconcern, although privately he was bubbling with pride.

But the rest of the ponies were in no mood for jokes. They fell upon Pippin with little snorts and nickers of delight, caressing her with their noses and nibbling her mane. Tattles was so overcome that he pranced in a kind of double pony jig up and down the wide passage.

Paul cleared his throat, arched his neck, and began to make a speech.

'Ladies and gentlemen, it is with overwhelming pleasure that I announce the return of Pippin to our assembly. Our heartfelt thanks and gratitude are due to –'

'Oh, stop it, Paul,' interrupted Tattles. 'Isn't it enough that we've got our Pippin back again? Jenny and Peter and Dragon and Cock Robin must know just how much we do thank them. And to celebrate the event, next time Jenny and Peter come we are going to have a meet of hounds at the stables.'

'A meet?' they all clamoured.

'Yes, a meet,' repeated Tattles impressively. 'To which everyone will turn out.'

'A meet! And we are going hunting?' exclaimed Jenny. 'I can't think of anything more wonderful.'

Rosina Copper

KITTY BARNE

Rosina Copper is a true story about the eventful life of an Argentine polo pony who fell on bad days after her tendons gave out. The people who buy her, in the incident described in this extract, spend the next part of their lives digging up her past history. In their good hands she becomes a great show-pony and show-jumper. They write a book about her life and sell it in aid of the Olympic show-jumping fund and Rosina Copper becomes a famous personality and is paraded at Harringay in the Horse of the Year show. By then she is thirty-five years old. A heart-warming story, beautifully written by Kitty Barne.

I found Meg talking away hard to a small man with a beaky red face, wearing about the oldest and baggiest riding breeches I'd ever seen. His hair where it showed under his cap was grey, but the peak was well pulled down and there wasn't much of it to be seen. He might have been any age. He was thin, a little bent and bow-legged, and altogether so horsy looking that one wanted to give him a lump of sugar. Just the sort of oldish man I like.

Meg gave me a welcoming wave – she was a welcoming sort of person, I could see, whether to animals or humans.

'Come on in and listen, Angie. This is Fred who was in our stables before I was born. He always knows all the horse gossip of the countryside and he's been telling me about a couple of ponies –'

'Lef' over, that's what they are,' wheezed Fred. His voice was the oldest part of him.

'Left over from what?' I asked.

'Those stables with the high-sounding name – Arabian Riding School, I think it was – have been sold up. They've been holding an auction in some private stables I used to know very well. They finished it up yesterday. But apparently there are two ponies that no one bought –'

'Forgotten, they was. Never put up –'

'Well, forgotten or unsold or whatever it was, Fred wants me to go over and see them. Shall we?'

The 'we' seemed to include me, so of course I said – nearly shouted, in fact – 'Do let's.'

'Not that I'm going to buy them. They can't be up to much and we've got all the horses we can do with as it is. But it's a horrible wet afternoon and we may as well do that as anything else.'

'*Do* let's,' I said again.

'You like meeting strange horses too, do you?' – she gave me a quick friendly look out of her blue eyes. 'All right. Come along then. Fred says the auctioneer is coming back at three to finish up, so we haven't much time. Put your pony in there.'

I pushed Happy Boy into the empty loose-box she pointed out while she got the car out. 'Coming, Fred?' she said, and he gave a grunt and clambered into the back. I hopped in beside her and off we went. Oh, what a bit of luck for me!

It wasn't far. In no time, it seemed, Fred was saying ''Ere you are, Mum,' and we were turning into a hundred yards or so of broad drive to find ourselves in front of most imposing stable gates thrown wide open, a clock tower with a clock (not going) in the arch over them.

They were, or had been, very grand and beautiful stables. The big house, empty for a long time, Meg said, stood back off the road, hidden away by trees, but if it lived up to its stables it must have been very grand and beautiful too; we never saw it. There was a big quadrangle full of doors, all of them tight shut; Meg drove into the stable yard and drew up, and I hopped out at once and took a run round it, looking into the windows and trying the doors. I couldn't see much because the glass was so dirty; however, here and there it was broken and I could look through and see the untidy mess they were all in after the auction. Then I came upon a door that opened and I found myself in a fine square harness room; quite empty, just one old very dusty saddle hanging up on the wall. They'd lit a fire in the open grate – for the auctioneer, I suppose – and the bonfire smell mixed with the leather-polish-horse smell and did its best to fill the room. But oh, *how* empty it was! The emptiness of empty stables is the worst kind, I said to myself – nothing at all left but the smell. All the same, these stables weren't really empty. Where were the ponies we'd come to see?

A doorway led to a flight of steep stairs – I'm always inquisitive about doors and stairs and paths and I thought I must just have a look. I brushed past a rusty old stove – oh, they'd kept themselves warm enough no doubt when the coachman lived there, but, my goodness, it was cold now. I flew up the stairs; the coachman's bedroom; a room beyond with a pale brownish paper that had once been pink and satiny and was still peppered all over with bright pink squares and oblongs and ovals where the coachman's wife had hung her pictures. Nothing at all in it but a roll of cracked linoleum. Beyond it another room, chocolate coloured, and a small low door that led into a big hayloft, still with a small mound of hay in one corner. There a black cat, quite a young cat with a shining carefully groomed black satin coat, came walking towards me, his tail straight up in the air like the mast of a little boat, his best manners on show.

He was a very smart well-fed looking cat; no shortage of mice in an empty stable, one could see that. He opened his yawning mouth, salmon pink like the coachman's wife's wallpaper, and gave a very small mew. I picked him up and he instantly settled down in my arms and started to purr. So down the stairs we went together.

'That all you've found?' said Meg; but she gave the cat's head an absent-minded stroke and scratched him a little under his chin. He purred louder, but she sighed. 'Oh, dear, how full of horse ghosts it is – and humans. I wonder what's become of the owner, the Squire, as we used to call him.'

'There don't seem to be any horses or ponies any-where,' I said.

'Well, there wouldn't be up those stairs, would there? We shall find ourselves bidding for the stable cat.'

She looked round the once beautiful yard, weeds shooting up between the cobble-stones, a mat of thick grass round the pump and trough, a broken half-door banging in the wind, and gave a sigh.

'Quite derelict. Very sad.'

'I did look into most of the loose boxes,' I said, trying to excuse myself for having gone exploring. 'They're empty.'

It began to rain quite hard, a cold sleety rain.

'Where's Fred?' I asked.

'Gone hunting. Like you. He thinks there's a man about.'

There was, and Fred had found him. We heard the clattering of boots, those heavy ones they wear when they're cleaning carriages, and the jangle of an empty pail, and there was Fred and an old man, a real ancient this time. His braces hung down outside breeches even baggier and older than Fred's, his leggings hadn't had a polish-up for months. He gave a vague touch of his cap with the remains of the manners that went with the stables. Then he set down his pail and began to work the pump handle; Fred made his way over to us.

'Well, Fred,' said Meg. 'Anything doing?'

'Auctioneer'll be along soonish.'

'But what's he going to auction?'

'Them two I told yer. They got to be sold without reserve – pay cost of stabling and food and that.'

'Where are they? Can we see them?'

The old man drawing water heard that; he held out a large key and waggled it at us.

'Good afternoon,' said Meg cheerfully, strolling over to him. 'You're looking after those two horses, are you?'

'No, I ain't.'

'Can we see them?'

The man nodded. 'No one bin near 'em since afore Christmas,' he said in a creaking, rusty voice, and clattered away with his pail, past a door that had once been blue and window-sills that still held the remains of window-boxes – a nice little house for a stable-man, I thought, as we followed him out of the yard.

There was an outhouse and that was where we were going. The door was tight shut and the old man set down his pail of water and fought with the lock, which his key refused to open.

There was a small window and Meg and I both tried to peer in while we waited, but we could see nothing through its spiders' webs and grime. The sleet was turning to snow and it was coming down with a wind like a knife behind it. 'Do you hear them?' whispered Meg, and I nodded. I could hear restless hoofs on the stone floor inside; one anyhow of the poor prisoners knew there was someone about.

'She's stuck,' grumbled the old man. 'They ain't bin taken outer the stable for weeks an' weeks,' and he looked at the key as if it was its fault.

'Ere, lemme 'ave a go at it,' wheezed Fred, and at last, muttering and quarrelling, together they turned it. In we went, thankful to get into shelter.

It was very dark. I stood there, blinking, and trying to distinguish what we were supposed to be looking at. I could just make out two loose boxes with a pony in each. As my eyes got used to the light I could see that one was a grey colt, a biggish pony, very dirty, rather frightened and inclined to kick. No one had bothered to clean him out, no one had dreamt of giving him any grooming. The other one looked even worse. She was a mare, a small, very thin, very miserable creature, her head turned into the corner away from us. A shiver ran over her now and again, otherwise she never moved.

'What's their history? D'you know?' asked Meg.

The old man knew nothing. He'd watered them and given them a bit of hay every day but no one had asked him to. He'd done it because, he said, some-one had to.

'Couldn't let 'em die, could I?' he demanded angrily.

'But they must belong to someone,' said Meg.

He said they didn't. Not to no one.

Fred chimed in.

'No good, either or which. Riding School don't own up to 'em. The colt ain't broken and the old mare's that wild no one can get on her.'

Wild? I couldn't believe it. She stood drooping in her corner, head down, eyes half shut, her three white stockings nearly hidden in the filthy straw. Anything less wild you could hardly imagine; she looked like nothing but a poor old sheep. Meg went up to her to give her a pat and speak to her, but all she did was to tremble from head to foot.

'Very nervous,' said Meg, and 'No good to anyone,' said the old man. And then we all trooped out again.

It began to snow quite hard and we as near as possible went home. However, we didn't quite because the auctioneer and his clerk arrived with a small boy in tow just as Meg was backing the car out. He was pretty annoyed at having to turn up again, and he grumbled away to us. Why these two animals weren't put in with the others he couldn't imagine. That

Riding School had hired these stables for the auction and then cleared out, taking the green parrot that belonged to them and, he'd been told, the contents of the till which didn't. No one's business to see to anything. And *what* weather. Was the fire lit in the harness room?

'No,' I said, 'it's not.'

He was cross and cold, but he was conscientious. We would have to wait a bit and see if anyone else turned up.

'Wait how long?' inquired Meg.

'An hour, say.'

The wind howled and the snow whirled round the derelict, magnificent stable yard. Meg and I got into the car again – Fred had disappeared, probably to sit by the fire of his new friend – the black cat still in my arms and still purring like a little dynamo. 'That's a very determined cat,' said Meg, looking at him. 'And he knows he's on to a good thing.'

'He's like a happy hot-water bottle,' I said.

But we didn't talk. Meg sat perfectly still and I could do nothing but dream of the stables as they had once been, horses' heads looking out of the half doors, grooms grooming and hissing, stable-boys washing carriage wheels, a tremendous clattering of hoofs when the carriage and pair went out with the coachman in white breeches on the box, a groom in a top hat beside him.

'*Lovely* stables,' I murmured to myself. 'They *could* be, I mean.'

'They *were*,' said Meg.

Presently the auctioneer put his head in at the car window and said to Meg:

'Nobody come. It's only you wants to buy 'em.'

'And I don't want to much. In fact I'm not sure I want to buy them at all. I couldn't see them in that awful dark stable.'

'I'll have them brought out for you,' said the auctioneer, getting on with the business. Then he added to the small boy, 'You cut along and find the old chap. He'll be about somewhere.'

So Meg and I got out of the car and waited.

'The colt's a bit uncertain,' said the auctioneer, trying to do his duty by the animals he had to sell. 'Don't feel sure they'll get him out. He's a good strong pony though – when you get him into condition. Fifteen hands.'

He was quite right. The colt wouldn't leave his box, he kicked at the very idea. He'd had no handling at all – anyone could see that.

'Will I bring out the mare?' asked the old man, fed up with the whole thing.

'May as well,' said Meg.

So there she stood, the poor little mare, shivering and shivering. A chestnut mare, they said, though you'd never have known what colour she was, her coat was so harsh and so dirty. The snow came down good and hard on to her and on us all. The auctioneer turned his collar up. 'Let's see her move,' he said perfunctorily. I could see he thought Meg quite mad to dream of buying either of these wretched creatures.

The old man walked the mare away – and a pair of very old down-and-outs they looked; she seemed almost too weak to stand, every rib showed through her miserable coat. However, he pulled himself to-gether and trotted her back – and a good thing he did, for, suddenly, a miracle happened. She threw her head up, pricked up her ears, and broke into the trot that one day was going to set the crowd cheering. Rosina Copper's trot. Courage, spirit, pride, she still had them all, and something in her told her to show them, even if it was the last thing she did on earth.

I heard a gasp of surprise. And a grunt from Fred. The auctioneer was looking the other way, the old man was rubbing his legs; they had noticed nothing.

Meg bought them both for £12.

'I'll throw in the cat,' said the auctioneer with a grin.

Meg went back for a horse-box and took the mare away that very night. I couldn't stay because I had to go home; it was the sort of afternoon that turns into night, and dark night too, before you know where you are. Happy and I had quite a time getting back in the snow. I asked them in the stable for some-thing hot and gave it to him before I fled up the back stairs myself and got into a frock just in time to follow the tea-tray into the drawing-room where Mother had tea.

'Have you been in long, darling?' she asked.

'Not very.'

'What have you been doing?'

I told her. I told her every word. She was as interested, almost, as I was myself.

'But why did she do it? What possessed your pony lady to *buy* the poor thing? She ought to have been given away and put into a home for old horses. What in the world is she going to do with her?'

'I don't know. It was the trot – the way she put her head up – the way she moved –'

'Yes, but what sort of mouth is she going to have? How old is she?'

'I don't know. I think quite old.'

'It seems to me quite mad. Where does she come from?'

'Nobody seems to know.'

'No name?'

'The old man said someone had called her Copper.'

'Copper? Why Copper?'

'I don't know.'

I didn't know anything, and that was the honest truth. But I'd got Mother thoroughly interested.

'I thought I'd go along tomorrow –'

'Yes. In the morning. She'll be expecting you, I daresay. Ask a lot of questions and tell me a lot more at lunch. They'll have cleaned the poor thing up a bit and you can tell me what her legs are like. And if they've got her to trot again –'

'Can I come down in riding things?'

'Yes. But don't start off before ten. You mustn't be a nuisance. I hope you won't be –' Mother again looked pretty doubtful.

'I won't be. I hope I'll be *useful*,' I cried fervently.

'You're so keen – I was just the same.'

'But so's Meg.'

'Meg?'

'She said I could call her that.'

'What's she like?'

And we settled down to talk and talk – the black ponies, the other horses, the stables, everything. It was such luck for me that Mother's a fairly horsy person and that she was interested in Copper from the very beginning.

As for Copper's companion in misery, he was given to a farmer who broke him to harness and gave him a busy but happy life on his farm. I never heard of him again.

The Black Brigade

W. J. GORDON

Before the motor car, funeral hearses were pulled by a pair or a team of black horses. The black horses were owned by a 'black master' who was what we would call a funeral director. Traffic in those days was all horse traffic, and traffic jams in London were just as common as they are now. In those days horses worked very hard; their lives were short. Note in this piece they are finished when they are ten years old. For a horse it wasn't necessarily a case of 'the good old days'. The best thing about it was that most people understood horses and they were treated with knowledge, though not necessarily with sympathy. Just like cars today.

Altogether there are about 700 of these black horses in London. They are all Flemish, and

come to us from the flats of Holland and Belgium
by way of Rotterdam and Harwich. They are the
youngest horses we import, for they reach us when
they are rising three years old, and take a year or
so before they get into full swing; in fact, they
begin work as what we may call the 'half-timers'
of the London horse-world. When young they cost
rather under than over a hundred guineas a pair, but
sometimes they get astray among the carriage folk,
who pay for them, by mistake of course, about
double the money. In about a year or more, when
they have got over their sea-sickness and other ail-
ments, and have been trained and acclimatized, they
fetch £65. each; if they do not turn out quite good
enough for first-class work they are cleared out to
the second-class men at about twenty-five guineas;
if they go to the repository they average £10.; if
they go to the knacker's they average thirty-five shillings, and they generally go there after six years'
work. Most of them are stallions, for Flemish geldings go shabby and brown. They are cheaper now
than they were a year or two back, for the ubiqui-
tous American took to buying them in their native
land for importation to the States, and thereby sent
up the price; but the law of supply and demand
came in to check the rise, and some enterprising indi-
vidual actually took to importing black horses here
from the States, and so spoilt the corner.

Here, in the East Road, are about eighty genuine

Flemings, housed in capital stables, well built, lofty, light, and well ventilated, all on the ground floor. Over every horse is his name, every horse being named from the celebrity, ancient or modern, most talked about at the time of his purchase, a system which has a somewhat comical side when the horses come to be worked together. Some curious traits of character are revealed among these celebrities as we pay our call at their several stalls. General Booth, for instance, is 'most amiable, and will work with any horse in the stud'; all the Salvationists 'are doing well', except Railton, 'who is showing too much blood and fire. Last week he had a plume put on his head for the first time, and that upset him.' Stead, according to his keeper, is 'a good horse, a capital horse – showy perhaps, but some people like the showy; he does a lot of work, and fancies he does more than he does. We are trying him with General Booth, but he will soon tire him out, as he has done others. He wouldn't work with Huxley at any price!' Curiously enough, Huxley 'will not work with Tyndall, but gets on capitally with Dr Barnardo'. Tyndall, on the other hand, 'goes well with Dickens', but has a decided aversion to Henry Ward Beecher. Morley works 'comfortably' with Balfour, but Harcourt and Davitt 'won't do as a pair anyhow'. An ideal team seems to consist of Bradlaugh, John Knox, Dr Adler, and Cardinal Manning. But the practice of naming horses after church and chapel dignitaries is being dropped owing to a superstition of the stable. 'All the horses,' the horsekeeper says, 'named after that kind of person go wrong somehow!' And so we leave Canon Farrar, and Canon Liddon, and Dr Punshon, and John Wesley and other lesser lights, to glance at the empty stalls of Abraham, Isaac, and Jacob, now 'out on a job', and meet in turn with Sequah and Pasteur, Mesmer and Mattei. Then we find ourselves amid a bewildering mixture of poets, politicians, artists, actors, and musicians.

'Why don't you sort them out into stables, and have a poet stable, an artist stable, and so on?'

'They never would stand quiet. The poets would never agree; and as to the politicians – well, you know what politicians are, and these namesakes of theirs are as like them as two peas!' And so the horses after they are named have to be changed about until they find fit companions, and then everything goes harmoniously. The stud is worked in sections of four; every man has four horses which he looks after and drives; under him being another man, who drives when the horses go out in pairs instead of in the team.

One would think these horses were big, black retriever dogs, to judge by the liking and understanding which spring up between them and their masters. It is astonishing what a lovable, intelligent animal a horse is when he finds he is understood. According to popular report these Flemish stallions are the most vicious and ill-tempered of brutes; but those who keep them and know them are of the very opposite opinion.

'I am not a horsey man,' said Mr Dottridge to us, 'but I have known this one particular class of horse all my life, and I say they are quite affectionate and good-natured, and seem to know instinctively what you say to them and what you want. If you treat them well they will treat you well. One thing they have is an immense amount of self-esteem, and that you have to humour. Of course I have to choose the horses, and I do not choose the vicious ones. I can tell them by the peculiar glance they give as they look round at me. The whole manner of the horse, like the whole manner of a man, betrays his character. Even his nose will tell you. People make fun of Roman noses; now I never knew a horse with a Roman nose to be ill-natured. The horse must feel that your will is stronger than his, and he does feel it instinctively. He knows at once if a man is afraid of him or even nervous, and no man in that state will ever do any good with a horse. Even when you are driving, if you begin to get nervous, the horse knows it instantly. He is in communication with you by means of the rein, and he is somehow sensible of the change in your mind, although perhaps you are hardly conscious of it. I have no doubt whatever but that you can influence a horse even when he is ill, by mere power of will. There are affinities between man and horse which are at present inexplicable, but they exist all the same.'

There is an old joke about the costermonger's donkey who looked so miserable because he had been

standing for a week between two hearse horses, and
had not got over the depression. The reply to this is
that the depression is mutual. The 'black family' has
always to be alone; if a coloured horse is stood in one
of the stalls, the rest of the horses in the stable will at
once become miserable and fretful. The experiment
has been tried over and over again, and always with
the same result; and thus it has come about that in the
black master's yards, the coloured horses used for ordinary draught work are always in a stable by themselves.

The funeral horse hardly needs description. The breed
has been the same for centuries. He stands about sixteen hands, and weighs between 12 and 13 cwt. The
weight behind him is not excessive, for the car does
not weigh over 17 cwt., and even with a lead coffin
he has the lightest load of any of our draught horses.
The worst roads he travels are the hilly ones to High-
gate, Finchley, and Norwood. These he knows well
and does not appreciate. In a few months he gets to
recognize all the cemetery roads 'like a book', and
after he is out of the bye streets he wants practically
no driving, as he goes by himself, taking all the proper
corners and making all the proper pauses. This knowledge of the road has its inconveniences, as it is often
difficult to get him past the familiar corner when he
is out at exercise. But of late he has had exercise
enough at work, and during the influenza epidemic
was doing his three and four trips a day, and the

funerals had to take place not to suit the convenience of the relatives, but the available horse-power of the undertaker. Six days a week he works, for after a long agitation there are now no London funerals on Sundays, except perhaps those of the Jews, for which the horses have their day's rest in the week.

To feed such a horse costs perhaps two shillings a day – it is a trifle under that, over the 700 – and his food differs from that of any other London horse. In his native Flanders he is fed a good deal upon slops, soups, mashes, and so forth; and as a Scotsman does best on his oatmeal, so the funeral horse, to keep in condition, must have the rye-bread of his youth. Rye-bread, oats, and hay form his mixture, with perhaps a little clover, but not much, for it would not do to heat him, and beans and such things are absolutely forbidden. Every Saturday he has a mash like other horses, but unlike them his mash consists, not of bran alone, but of bran and linseed in equal quantities. What the linseed is for we know not; it may be, as a Life Guardsman suggested to us, to make his hair glossy, that beautiful silky hair which is at once his pride and the reason of his special employment, and the sign of his delicate, sensitive constitution.

National Velvet

ENID BAGNOLD

National Velvet is the classic pony book, the only one there is. It is still in print after forty years. I bought it when I was ten, from a railway bookstall while coming home from school, and have loved it ever since. It is about Velvet, the butcher's daughter who dreams of horses, and all her dreams come true. As well as being left five horses in Mr Cellini's will, Velvet draws the winning ticket in a raffle for a wild piebald horse. Disguised as a Russian jockey, she rides the piebald to win the Grand National. What a plot! The characterizations and writing are superb.

Velvet's dreams were blowing about the bed. They were made of cloud but had the shapes of horses. Sometimes she dreamt of bits as women dream of jewellery. Snaffles and straights and pelhams and twisted pelhams were hanging, jointed and still in the shadows of a stable, and above them went up the straight damp oiled lines of leathers and cheek straps. The weight of a shining bit and the delicacy of the leathery above it was what she adored. Sometimes she walked down an endless cool alley in summer, by the side of the gutter in the old red-brick floor. On her left and right were open stalls made of dark wood and the buttocks of the bay horses shone like mahogany all the way down. The horses turned their heads to look at her as she walked. They had black manes hanging like silk as the thick necks turned. These dreams blew and played round her bed in the night and the early hours of the morning.

She got up while the sisters were sleeping and all the room was full of book-muslin and canaries singing. 'How they can sleep! . . .' she said wonderingly when she became aware of the canaries singing so madly. All the sisters lay dreaming of horses. The room seemed full of the shapes of horses. There was almost a dream-smell of stables. As she dressed they were stirring, shifting and tossing in white heaps beneath their cotton bedspreads. The canaries screamed in a long yellow scream, and grew madder. Then Velvet left the room and softly shut the door and passed down into the silence of the cupboard-stairway.

In her striped cotton dress with a cardigan over it she picked up the parcel of steak that had been left on the kitchen table and drank the glass of milk with a playing card on the top of it that Mrs Brown had left her overnight. Then she got a half packet of milk chocolate from the string drawer, and went out to saddle Miss Ada.

In the brilliance of a very early summer morning they went off together, Miss Ada's stomach rumbling with hunger. Velvet fed her from a bag of oats she had brought with her up on the top of the hill. There were spiders' webs stretched everywhere across the gorse bushes.

Coming down over the rolling grass above Kingsworthy, Velvet could see the feathery garden looking like tropics asleep down below. Old Mr Cellini by a miracle grew palms and bananas and mimosa in his. Miss Ada went stabbing and sliding down the steep hillside, hating the descent, switching her tail with vexation.

Velvet tied Miss Ada to the fence, climbed it and crept through the spiny undergrowth into the foreign garden. There was not a sound. Not a gardener was about. The grass like moss, spongy with dew so that each foot sank in and made a black print which filled with water. Then she looked up and saw that the old gentleman had been looking at her all the time.

He had on a squarish hat and never took his eyes off her. He was standing by a tree. Velvet's feet went down in the moss as she stood. His queer hat was wet, and there was dew on the shoulders of his ancient black frockcoat which buttoned up to the neck; he looked like someone who had been out all the night.

Raising one black-coated arm he rubbed his lips as though they were stiff, and she could see how frail he was, unsteady, wet.

'What have you come to do?' he said in a very low voice.

'Sir?'

He moved a step forward and stumbled.

'Are you staying? Going up to the house?'

'The house.'

'Stay here,' he said, in an urgent tone which broke.

Velvet dropped her own eyes to her parcel, for she knew he was looking at her and how his eyeballs shone round his eyes.

'How did you come?' (at last). She looked up. There was something transparent about his trembling face.

'On our pony,' she said. 'I rode. She's tied to the fence. There's some meat here for the cook, to leave at the back door.'

'Do you like ponies?' said the rusty voice.

'Oh . . . yes. We've only the one.'

'Better see mine,' said the old gentleman in a different tone.

He moved towards her, and as they walked he rested one hand on her shoulder. They walked till they came to the open lawns and passed below some fancy bushes.

He stopped. And Velvet stopped.

'. . . if there was anything you wanted very much,' he said, as though to himself.

Velvet said nothing. She did not think it was a question.

'I'm very much too old,' said the old gentleman. 'Too old. What did you say you'd brought?'

'Meat,' said Velvet. 'Rump.'

'Meat,' said the old gentleman. 'I shan't want it. Let's see it.'

Velvet pulled the dank parcel out of her bag.

'Throw it away,' said the old gentleman, and threw it into a bush.

They walked on a few paces.

Something struck her on the hip as she walked. It was when his coat swung out. He looked down too, and unbuttoned his coat and slowly took it off. Without a word he hung it over his arm, and they walked on again, he in his black hat and black waistcoat and shirt-sleeves.

'Going to the stables,' said he. 'Why, are you fond of horses?'

There was something about him that made Velvet feel he was going to say goodbye to her. She fancied he was going to be carried up to Heaven like Elisha.

'Horses,' he said. 'Did you say you had horses?'

'Only an old pony, sir.'

'All my life I've had horses. Stables full of them. You like 'em?'

'I've seen your chestnut,' said Velvet. 'Sir Pericles. I seen him jump.'

'I wish he was yours, then,' said the old gentleman, suddenly and heartily. 'You said you rode?'

'We've on'y got Miss Ada. The pony. She's old.'

'Huh!'

'Not so much *old*,' said Velvet hurriedly. 'She's obstinate.'

He stopped again.

'Would you tell me what you want most in the world? . . . Would you tell me that?'

He was looking at her.

'Horses,' she said. 'Sir.'

'To ride on? To own for yourself?'

He was still looking at her, as though he expected more.

'I tell myself stories about horses,' she went on, desperately fishing at her shy desires. 'Then I can dream about them. Now I dream about them every night. I want to be a famous rider, I should like to carry dispatches, I should like to get a first at Olympia, I should like to ride in a great race, I should like to have so many horses that I could walk down between the two rows of loose boxes and ride what I chose. I would have them all under fifteen hands, I like chestnuts best, but bays are lovely too, but I don't like blacks.'

She ran out the words and caught her breath and stopped.

At the other end of the golden bushes the gardener's lad passed in the lit, green gap between two rhododendron clumps with a bodge on his arm. The old gentleman called to him. Then he walked onwards across the grass and Velvet and the gardener's boy followed after. They neared a low building of old brick with a square cobbled yard outside it. The three passed in under the arched doorway.

'Five,' said the old gentleman. 'These are my little horses. I like little ones too.' He opened the gate of the first loose box and a slender chestnut turned slowly towards him. It had a fine, artistic head, like horses which snort in ancient battles in Greece.

'Shake hands, Sir Pericles,' said the old gentleman, and the little chestnut bent its knee and lifted a slender foreleg a few inches from the ground.

'But I've no sugar,' said the old gentleman. 'You must do your tricks for love today.'

He closed the door of the loose box.

In the next box was a grey mare.

'She was a polo pony,' he said, 'belonged to my son.' He still wore his hat, black waistcoat, and shirt sleeves. He looked at the gardener's boy. 'I need not have bothered you,' he said. 'Of course the grooms are up.' But the gardener's boy, not getting a direct order, followed them gently in the shadow of the stables.

The grey mare had the snowy grey coat of the brink of age. All the blue and dapple had gone out of her, and her eyes burned black and kind in her white face. When she had sniffed the old gentleman she turned her back on him. She did not care for stable-talk.

In the next loose box was a small pony, slim and strong, like a miniature horse. He had a sour, suspicious pony face. There were two more loose boxes to come and after that a gap in the stables. Far down the corridor between the boxes Velvet could see where the big horses stood. Hunters and carriage horses and cart horses.

The gardener's boy never stirred. The old gentleman seemed suddenly tired and still.

He moved and pulled a piece of paper from the pocket of his waistcoat. 'Get me a chair,' he said very loud. But before the boy could move a groom came running swiftly with a stable chair.

The old gentleman sat down and wrote. Then he looked up.

'What's your name?' he said and looked at Velvet.

'Velvet Brown,' said Velvet.

'Velvet Brown,' he said and tapped his pencil on his blue cheek. Then wrote it down. 'Sign at the bottom, boy,' he said to the gardener's boy, and the boy knelt down and wrote his careful name. 'Now you sign too,' he said to the groom.

The old gentleman rose and Velvet followed him out into the sunlight of the yard. 'Take that paper,' he said to her, 'and you stay there,' and he walked from her with his coat on his arm.

He blew himself to smithereens just round the corner. Velvet never went to look. The grooms came running.

The warm of the brick in the yard was all she had to hold on to. She sat on it and listened to the calls and exclamations. 'Gone up to Heaven, Elisha,' she

thought, and looked up into the sky. She would like
to have seen him rising, sweet and sound and happy.

In the paper in her hand she read that five of his
horses belonged to her.

Taking the paper, avoiding the running and the
calling of the household, she crept back through the
garden to Miss Ada. When she got home she could not
say what had happened, but cried and trembled and was
put to bed and slept for hours under the golden screams
of the canaries. At four o'clock Mally burst in and cried:

'They've drawn! They've drawn! We've got the piebald!'

'Whose ticket?' said Velvet faintly.

'Yours, oh yours. Are you ill?'

'Whur's the little chap?' said Mr Croom, 'Donald?'

'I'm here,' said Donald through the half-open yard
door.

'I got silver an' gold for you,' said Mr Croom.

'More'n he deserves,' said Mrs Brown.

Donald came in brightly with his sweet smile.

'Silver an' gold,' said Mr Croom, holding out a net
bag full of chocolate coins covered in silver and gold
paper. 'Foreign,' he said, 'Dutch stuff. But Donald
won't care.'

'Say thank you,' said Mr Brown.

'Thank you,' said Donald, with his heart in his
face. He took the bag and wandered away.

'Fine chap,' said Mr Croom.

'Cup of coffee, Mr Croom ?' said Mr Brown.

'If you're making any.' Mr Croom peered through the street window. 'Quite a stir in the village.'

'Yes,' said Mr Brown.

''Strordinary thing,' said Mr Croom. 'Like a tale.'

'Yes,' said Mr Brown again. 'Took to Velvet, I suppose.'

'Ever seen him before, Velvet?' said Mr Croom.

'Yes,' said Velvet faintly. 'Once. At the Lingdown Horse Show.'

'Better leave her,' said Mrs Brown. 'Turns her stomach.'

'Well, well . . .' said Mr Croom regretfully. 'Yes.'

Mr Cellini swam across the ceiling, frailer than memory, like a cobweb.

Mr Brown rose again and looked at his watch on the sideboard. 'Should be here,' he said.

'Where's your gold and silver bag?' said Velvet suddenly to Donald.

'I put it away,' said Donald.

'Don't you want it?' said Mr Croom, hurt.

'No,' said Donald. 'I might want it some day.'

'What you got there instead?'

'It's my spit bottle,' said Donald, holding up a medicine bottle on a string.

He walked a little farther into the room and dangled the bottle, showing a little viscous fluid in the bottom. 'That's my spit,' he said.

'He's collecting his spit,' said Velvet.

Donald applied his mouth at the top and with difficulty dribbled a little more spit into the neck.

'D'you let him do those sort o' things?' said Mr Brown to Mrs Brown.

'Take it outside,' said Mrs Brown. 'Here's your coffee, Mr Croom.'

Edwina, Malvolia and Meredith burst the street door open with the crowd behind their shoulders. 'Over the hill! You can see them!' Meredith panted, and all three disappeared.

Mrs Brown picked up Donald, his spit bottle swinging. 'Put your cardigan on,' she said to Velvet. 'Keep warm an' you'll be all right.'

They all went out, the crowd following them, and turned up the chalk road.

'Where's Mi?' said Velvet suddenly.

'Got a half-dozen sheep to fetch,' said Mr Brown. 'Be here any minute.'

'Poor Mi,' said Velvet, and walked on, wrapt with happiness.

Over the brow of the hill five horses moved down towards them.

'Ther's three grooms. My word, ther's three of them,' said Mally, who had joined the procession. The grooms were walking the horses, two horses to a groom, then one alone at the back. As they reached the foot of the grass slope and stepped on to the flashing chalky road in the sun, the black crêpe could be seen on the arm of each walking groom. They were bowler-hatted and round each bowler a band of crêpe was tied. The head groom, walking in front with the grey mare and Sir Pericles, had a rosy face and a fine black coat of good cloth. The others wore dark grey.

The horses were halted at the entrance to the village.

The head groom produced a slip of paper. 'Miss Velvet Brown?' he asked. Mr Brown stepped forward, Velvet close behind. Her thin face shone, smile alight, frock ballooned under cardigan, legs bare and scratched. 'I'm Velvet,' she said.

She walked up to Sir Pericles, transfigured, touched him gently on his neck, took the rein from the groom.

'We'll go down to the house,' she said softly. 'I'll lead this one home.'

'Better let me,' said the groom. Velvet stared at him, shook her head, and walked on leading the shining horse.

'Daft today,' said Mr Brown to the groom.

'Mind she don't let him go then,' said the groom.

The procession went on, Velvet first with her horse, Mr Brown at her elbow, the horses and the village people following. 'Keep the boys back! Don't let them frighten the horses!' said the old head groom.

'Keep back there,' said Mr Croom mildly, and the boys ran and skipped. Edwina and Malvolia and Meredith went ahead, turning to look over their shoulders.

'Better stop!' called Edwina.

The procession drew up and halted as it reached the street. Half a dozen sheep had arrived unexpectedly from a farm for the slaughter-house, and Mi was

striving to get the last three in. He ran about in his
Sunday clothes, put on for the arrival of the horses.
They could hear him cursing. The three sheep
skipped, butted and ran. 'Yer poor slut,' yelled Mi to
the last one, bounding like a hare to keep it out of the
main road. He turned it, and the last of the sheep
went dingily behind the great wooden door. With the
clatter of delicate feet on brick the horses moved on till
they reached the sunny square before the cottage.

Donald was swinging his bottle before the door.
He had not kept up with the procession.

'Keep that child in!' called Mr Brown. But Donald
swung his bottle gently, and Mrs Brown did no more
than lay a finger on his head.

The horses were drawn up facing the doorway and
the second groom took over the bunch of leather
reins. They ran like soft straps of silk over his fingers,
narrow, polished, and flexible.

'Better take this into the house and read it over,'
suggested the head groom to Mr Brown, handing
him a typewritten sheet.

Mr Brown glanced at it and called to Velvet. Together they went in at the door and sat down at the
little fern table inside. Mr Brown pushed the ferns
gently to one side and laid out the sheet.

'One chestnut gelding. 14 hands. Seven years
old, *Sir Pericles*. 1 snaffle bit, bridle, noseband
and standing martingale. 1 Ambrose saddle,
leathers and stirrups. 1 pair webbing girths.'

And underneath this Velvet wrote 'Velvet Brown'.

'One grey polo pony. Mare. 15 hands. Nine years old. *Mrs James*. 1 straight pelham, etc. . . . martingale . . . soft saddle and sewn girths.

And underneath Velvet wrote 'Velvet Brown'.

'1 child's pony, chestnut. 12.2 hands. Gelding. *George*. Snaffle bit and double bit. Soft saddle and sewn girths, etc.'

And Velvet wrote 'Velvet Brown'.

'1 cob pony, for hacking or cart. 13.3 hands, dark bay gelding. *Fancy*. 1 double bit, etc. . . . old leather saddle, and harness for cart.'

'Velvet Brown'.

'1 Dartmoor filly, two years old, unbroken. 11 hands. Halter only. *Angelina*.'

'Velvet Brown'.

When Velvet had written her name for the fifth time, carefully, in ink, and with her breath held tight, her father touched her arm, and they both returned to the sunlight of the street. Mr Brown gave the paper to the head groom.

'What are you doing with them straight away?' said the groom.

'Turning them into a field of mine,' said Mr Brown.

The groom hesitated. 'Warm weather, but they've none on 'em been out at night yet. Won't hurt the little filly.'

'They'll have to be out now,' said Mr Brown, with a slight rise of voice, as though he were being dictated to.

'Will they eat sugar?' said Mally.

'All except the grey mare,' said the groom. 'She likes apple.'

Mally brought sugar out of her cotton pocket. Meredith went for an apple.

'Shall you be selling them, sir?' said the groom, a little hesitatingly to Mr Brown.

'They're mine!' said Velvet suddenly.

'We've not decided anything,' said Mr Brown. Velvet's soul became several sizes too large for her, her mouth opened, and she struggled with speech. Mrs Brown's hand fell on her shoulder, and her soul sank back to its bed.

'I suppose you are fixed up with a man?' said the head groom tentatively. 'I have a place myself, but ...' he made a gesture towards the other two grooms.

'I'm a butcher,' said Mr Brown firmly. 'My girl goes and gets herself five horses. Five! We've seven all told, with that piebald. If she has to have horses she must look after 'em. We've fields in plenty, and there's oats in the shed, and I've four girls all of an age to look after horses. Beyond that I won't go. I'll have no fancy stables here. I'm a plain man and a butcher, and we've got to live.'

'Eh, yes,' said the little old rosy head groom. 'Shall we unsaddle them and turn them into the field for you?'

'Saddles'll have to go in the slaughter-house,' said Mr Brown. 'Through with them sheep yet?' he said to Mi.

'Ain't begun,' said Mi.

'Well then, you can put the saddles in the sun here on the wood rail, and lead 'em to the field in the bridles. Head collars they have on 'em. P'raps you'd better leave the bridles here.'

The head groom went up to the girths of Sir Pericles, but Velvet's thin hand was on his arm. 'I'm going to try them all first,' she said.

Mr Brown heard what she said, though he made no sign. He looked at Donald, then at his wife. She made no sign either.

'Fetch your gold sweets now!' said Mr Brown heavily and with unreality to Donald, tweaking his chin, and retired from the whole scene towards the slaughter-house.

'Let's go round to the field,' said Velvet, with confidence, to the groom.

'Wait a bit,' said Mrs Brown. 'You'll have a little something first. Edwina, there's that bottle of port. Bring it out. And glasses. Mr Croom you'll join too, a drop won't do anybody any harm.'

Edwina and Mally brought out the fern table, a tin one, the sacred table that was never moved.

Velvet as the heroine, Edwina as the eldest, the

head groom as the guest, and Mrs Brown as the hostess sat down at the table and sipped a sip from the thick glasses of port. The village stood round at a respectful distance and Mally and Meredith walked among the horses. Sir Pericles drooped his neck and nuzzled by the head groom's pockets. The second grooms shared a glass between them. Then they all went up to the field to try the horses.

Velvet mounted Sir Pericles. She had ridden Miss Ada for eight years, hopped her over bits of brushwood and gorse-bushes, and trotted her round at the local gymkhana. Once she had ridden a black pony belonging to the farmer at Pendean. She had a natural seat, and her bony hands gathered up the reins in a tender way. But she had never yet felt reins that had a trained mouth at the end of them, and, as she cantered up the slope of the sunny field with the brow of the hill and the height of the sky in front of her, Sir Pericles taught her in three minutes what she had not known existed. Her scraggy, childish fingers obtained results at a pressure. The living canter bent to right or left at her touch. He handed her the glory of command.

When she slid to the ground by the side of the head groom she was speechless, and leant her forehead for a second on the horse's flank.

'You ride him a treat,' said the groom. 'You done a bit of riding.'

'Never ridden anything but her old pony,' said Mi, his hair rising in pride.

'The mare here's harder,' said the groom. 'Excitable and kind of tough.'

He shot Velvet's light body and cotton frock into this second saddle. Her sockless feet, leather-shod, nosed for the stirrups. The groom shortened the leathers till they would go no more, and then tied knots in them. Mrs James, the mare, broke into a sweat at once. She flirted her ears wildly back and forwards, curved her grey neck, shook her bit, gave backward glances with her black eyes, like polished stones in her pale face.

'Mind! She don't start straight! She'll leap as she starts, and then she'll settle. She was Mr Frank's polo pony an' she's not really nervous but she's keen.'

There was scum on the mare's neck already, and the reins carved it off on to the leather as she shook her head. Mrs Brown, holding Donald by the wall, watched quietly. Edwina, Mally and Merry sat on the gate.

'Hang on!' said the groom, and let go. Mrs James, with a tremendous leap, started up the field. Her nostrils were distended, her ears pricked with alarm. She thought she carried a ghost. She could not feel anything on her back, yet her mouth was held. Velvet, whose hand had slipped down to the pommel of the saddle at the first leap, settled more steadily and lifted her hand to the reins. Mrs James snorted as she cantered, like a single-cylindered car. She was not difficult to ride once the first start had been weathered. They rounded the field together; then Velvet got up on the pony George. George threw her as soon as her cotton frock touched his back.

'Get up again,' said the head groom and held the pony tighter.

'Walk him, walk him,' said the groom warningly. 'Trot before you canter or he'll buck!'

George stuck his head out in an ugly line, and Velvet tried gently to haul him in. The whites of his eyes gleamed and his nose curled. He snatched at the bit when he felt her pressure and stretched his neck impatiently. Velvet's lips could not tighten, there was too much gold; but her eyes shone. She twirled the ends of the long reins and caught him hard, first on one shoulder, then on the other.

'She'll be off!' said Edwina.

'Not she!' said Mi. 'It's what he's asking for.'

George curved his neck and flirted archly with his bit, then trotted smartly back to the gate. Velvet dismounted and turned to Fancy, the cob.

Fancy was no faster than Miss Ada, and somewhat her build. He trotted round the field sedately.

'That's the lot,' said the groom. 'The filly's not broke.'

'I must try George again,' said Velvet.

'You bin on the lot,' said Mrs Brown. 'Come home now.'

'But Merry and Mally . . .'

'The horses'll get all of a do,' said the head groom, 'if they get too many on 'em. Better let them graze now, and tomorrow they'll be more themselves.'

The horses were turned loose and the saddlery carried back to the slaughter-house, where it was straddled over iron hook-brackets among the sheep's bodies.

Jump for Joy

PAT SMYTHE

In her time Pat Smythe was a household name, much like Harvey Smith. But, unlike Harvey, Pat was a mere slip of a schoolgirl. She jumped for Britain before she was twenty on a horse she had broken in and schooled as a child.

Of course, there was riding and jumping – always jumping. First, there was the jumping with cousin Sheila. We would organize contests on the lawn, hurdling deck-chairs and fruit boxes – using only our legs – and although it was an innocent enough pastime we invested it, I thought, with at least one original flavour: we carefully timed each other around the home-made course in the pretence that our game was a major international competition. Sheila was young enough to be delighted with it all, and I was by no means old enough to feel too superior for such pranks.

All the time, I rode and trained and jumped my ponies – in particular the two which I soon began entering for gymkhana and country show events: Fireworks and Malta. I joined the Cotswold Pony Club, enjoyed their trail rides, hunter trials, and rallies, suffered a thousand minor falls, and learned a little more each day. One afternoon, when a half-dozen friends came to tea, I was being a shade too exhibitionist as I entertained them with a display of trick riding on Malta, the chestnut mare. In the middle of a dramatic and perilous movement – brilliantly sensational, I daresay, if it had succeeded – where I was sitting back to front on Malta's loins, she decided to register an objection, bucked me violently over her head and I sailed six yards through the air to land in a soft pile of lettuces which had been carefully laid ready for the market.

News of the most serious fall I foolishly kept from Mother and Father, to my ultimate cost. Not far from the house, I was schooling Fireworks over a solid fence (essential for good schooling with any horse) and we were both feeling very satisfied with the experience. Suddenly, however, Fireworks crashed the top of the fence and fell, landing fairly heavily on top of me. My ribs ached as I rode her home, and after ensuring that the mare was none the worse for the accident, I entered the house. Guilt, or pain, or both, must have been writ large on my face, for Mother looked sharply at me and said with some suspicion:

'*What* have *you* been doing, young lady?'

'Nothing at all, just playing,' I lied. 'But I've got an awful tummy ache. I think I'll go to bed.'

Mother looked surprised, but said nothing, and after I had washed and undressed she brought a glass of hot milk and a biscuit to my room. I told her I felt a little better, kissed her good night, and she left. When she tiptoed quietly into the room three hours later, I pretended to be sleeping, though in fact I was wide awake – with pain. I did not dare reveal that Fireworks had thrown me, for I was convinced that Mother would at once forbid me to jump solid fences, and since I was already planning to enter competitions involving fences just as solid, I kept the discomfort to myself for the three weeks that elapsed before the pain in my ribs finally subsided. Years later, when I was touring abroad and jumping in international events, I still received an occasional twinge of pain in the same spot. A doctor told me I had probably damaged a rib that day at Crickley, and prompt medical attention would almost certainly have set it right in next to no time. So perhaps it is better to face the music – even at the age of thirteen.

Then came Finality – the foal of a milk-cart mare and a thoroughbred stallion – who in the years to come was to bring me more joy, thrills, laughter, and heartbreak than any horse I had known.

Finality was really the outcome of a sensational scene which took place one autumn day in the High Street at Tunbridge Wells, where a milkman's horse kicked her cart to pieces before a crowd of astonished housewives and shopkeepers. Kitty, the milk horse, was a greedy, excitable, spirited mare who tended to be a thorn in the side of the local tradesman who owned her. On this day, she went berserk, bucked and kicked her way from one side of the busy street to the other, smashed the cart, sent bottles flying, and spread an ocean of milk all around her. Among the spectators of this drama was a farmer with a sense of humour, and when he observed the milkman's fast-growing despair he neatly stepped in with a commercial proposition. Gazing at the destruction, the milkman was in a mood almost to *pay* for Kitty being taken off his hands, and so the astute farmer got her at a bargain price. Kitty was taken home, where she was put to a thoroughbred. Time marched on, and she produced three foals.

Finality was the third – and the last, for Kitty died soon after her birth from the little weakness which was certain, sooner or later, to be her undoing: over-eating, on this occasion a surfeit of lettuce leaves. Her foal, who was therefore brought up on the bottle, eventually found her way into the keeping of our old friend Johnny Traill and he it was who sent her to us at Crickley when the war had run half its course; it was early in 1943.

Now a three-year-old, Finality arrived in the black-out. The Crickley telephone had buzzed at eleven o'clock when Mother was climbing into bed; nothing had gone right that day, Father having been in great pain and in need of much attention. Mother had spent half the previous night at his bedside, had coped with a series of maddening domestic accidents, and was wholly exhausted. She was almost in tears when a voice at the end of the line said:

'Mrs Smythe . . . Cheltenham Station speaking . . . a horse has arrived for you . . . we can't keep it here all night, so would you come and collect as soon as possible?'

Mother dressed, saddled Fireworks (we had no car at that time), and rode, half asleep, the nine miles to Cheltenham. Midnight had come and gone when she picked up the three-year-old and began the long homeward trek. When they reached Leckhampton Hill, the trouble started. This was the location of a 'haunted' house, where there had been at the beginning of the war a gruesome murder – an unsavoury 'torso' crime, with limbs chopped off and buried beneath floorboards. Despite the amused contempt of our rationalist friends, we had learned through bitter experience that the horses would never pass this house without a show of nervous excitement. And so it was on this night of all nights. As they came to the haunted house Mother's pony gave a whinny of alarm, swung round, and tossed her head, and caused Mother to lose her hold on the leading rein attached to the new three-year-old. A second later the horse bolted, and Mother gave chase. It took her half an hour to catch up with the frightened newcomer; it was four a.m. when they reached home.

Next day, Mother told us the story of her adventure in the small hours, showed me the new horse, and concluded:

'So you see, she's a proper Late Night Final.'

Thereafter we called her Finality, or Final, and started the difficult process of breaking her in. Difficult indeed with Finality, because she was a gawky green frame of a creature who inspired roars of derision from our friends when they learned that I intended making her my show-jumper. One of our visitors, Jock Houston-Boswell, the owner of Rondo and other racehorses, laughed heartily at the sight of Finality and called her 'The Box'. Child that I was, I was hurt and furious, and wanted to box his ears.

I found that Finality was a most uncomfortable ride, for she seemed not so much one horse as two halves joined by a long back. So many things were wrong about her: she needed a great deal of circling and schooling and would always 'lead' with the opposite foreleg-to-hind-leg; her weight was all in front, and I had to teach her to carry her head higher; dismounted, she would never stand still when I held her, but would walk incessantly around me; brought up on the bottle, she retained an affectionate but disconcerting habit of pushing me in the stomach, presumably anticipating her milk.

So much that was wrong . . . but so much that was utterly right. She was sensitive and friendly, responsive and humorous, disobedient, yet able and willing to learn. Perhaps it was the occasional flash of almost human eccentricity, as well as her later brilliance, that brought us so close. When, for example, she was turned out in the field near the chicken run, I would often catch her stealing the boiled potatoes or vegetables or kitchen scraps thrown down for the fowls; and if, as usually happened, the scraps were flavoured with a certain well-known poultry spice, Final would attack her illicit meals with even greater relish, and would then gaze a trifle sheepishly over the fence – her mouth enlivened like a clown's with a wide red rim. At all events I loved her dearly, and was convinced from the start that, box-like or not, she would develop into a show-jumper of the first class.

Although, during the summer, I worked Finality and devoted as much time as possible to her training, it was not with her that I began the round of Red Cross Gymkhanas that became my wartime training ground. This was a time for Fireworks, the fast, brilliant pony who came from Uncle Gordon. Fireworks adored the gymkhanas and went with immense gaiety into everything she tackled. At Musical Chairs she was a genius. The game is not so different from its orthodox counterpart at a children's party, except that you are mounted on horseback, cantering around the ring, galloping to the centre when the music stops, dismounting and sitting on a chair, or a bench or log. Our polo pony schooling gave us powerful advantages, since all polo ponies are trained for riding with one hand, and it was thus that I was able to ride Fireworks and other horses. She soon acquired an uncanny sense of instantaneous speed at the moment when the music ceased, but she was almost equally handy in a hundred and one other gymkhana events – potato races, where you dash to a post, lift a potato from the top, gallop away and drop it into a bucket; musical hats, and sacks, and mystery races; relays and Red Cross 'rescues', and the rest. Fireworks was so brilliant that she could carry off the prize not only for juvenile contests but for such things as the Open Musical Chairs. The bob-apple race was another favourite, though I always feared that Fireworks would extract the apple from the bucket before me!

Before long I was joyfully putting a pound a week into my Post Office savings account; it was always a rule that I pay my own entry fees at the gymkhanas – usually half-a-crown for each entry – and so it was more than ever essential that I should win enough to continue with them. The first prize was invariably one pound. Malta, the chestnut mare, was also a winner of many gymkhana prizes, but Fireworks was unquestionably the star turn.

Within a few months of her arrival, Finality seemed ripe for some jumping experience in public. I was fourteen, had moved from the grammar school and gone as a weekly boarder to St Michael's School at Cirencester. My chief desire was to race home at week-ends to ride Finality. During dozens of outings, on which we jumped everything we encountered, Final's ability grew rapidly. Mother had warned me to be careful not to hustle her into trying to do too much and so damaging her confidence, and so I would keep her all the time to small obstacles which she could jump freely and in good style. Our harmony developed as I schooled her, cantered her in small circles over small jumps, and gradually saw that she was learning to accept control and respond to those vital forms of encouragement which are known to a rider as 'aids'. Finality absorbed the notion that jumping was all in the day's work and not an ordeal to get excited about. Eventually I entered her for her first competition.

It was a Red Cross gymkhana run by Mother, at Witcombe near Crickley, where one spectacle was to be a display of trick jumping. We found, however, that there were not enough horses belonging to other people, aside from our own ponies. So the children of the pony club were mounted for the most part on our horses from Crickley; one of my friends rode Finality, another took Malta, a third rode Pixie, and I was on Fireworks. There was a big crowd of spectators, all intrigued by the array of trick fences. We set the ball rolling – six young riders, all from the Cotswold Pony Club – by jumping a deck-chair in which a dummy reclined. Next came a cleverly constructed hurdle – with an arch of roses by way of decoration. Then a washing-line hung with everything from babies' nappies to frilly underwear and a pair of men's long pants. Then a tea-table, neatly laid for four. Now the excitement was rising. A large bed containing a stuffed dummy of Adolf Hitler faced us. We jumped him successfully and headed for the final obstacle – fire. Jumping in pairs we sailed across a pole hung with blazing straw, and the crowd was highly appreciative. Finally, with one other girl, I galloped for the bed, from which we pulled out Hitler, raced with him back to the blazing pole and dropped him mercilessly into the fire amid cries of triumph. The grand climax came with the entire team forming a V-for-Victory sign. It was a pleasant way to raise money for a good cause.

But Finality quite disgraced herself in this, her first public appearance. She came to the washing-line, jumped it, failed to pick up her hind legs, and tore down the rope, scattering nappies and lingerie all over the ring while the crowd roared with laughter.

Soon afterwards, I decided to take Finality on a round of local shows, combining these with gymkhanas where I was still riding Fireworks. Mother was extremely co-operative, told me she was now confident in my ability to take care of myself *and* the horses, and allowed me to ride off to country shows often twenty, thirty, even forty miles away. I felt very grown-up.

To reach the more distant places I would start the day before, riding Fireworks, leading Finality, and carrying on my back a rucksack with food, toothbrush, and pyjamas. As a rule there would be friends on the way with whom I could spend the night, but on several trips I had to stay at small farms, and once we camped – the three of us – under trees beside a stream. They were wonderful days, often passed, conversationally, with no one save the horses, and at the shows I could always rely on Fireworks paying our way with her winnings. Indeed, she had to – since whenever I entered Finality for an Open jumping competition the fee was no less than a pound, which was something of a strain compared with the half-crown I laid out for Fireworks in her gymkhana events. And in the jumping, Finality was undistinguished for some time, winning little or nothing; but I was far from disappointed, for we were both winning experience at every step.

One of these summer excursions, alone with Fireworks, brought another kind of experience – one which I shall never forget, perhaps because it was the first of its kind, and at fourteen and a half the first of most things is engraved with importance. We had been to a show some thirty miles away and we were both in high spirits after Fireworks had romped home with two victories. The night was strikingly beautiful and I decided to ride home, calculating that I could reach Crickley by midnight, and hoping to creep to bed without disturbing the household. We set off, and by eleven o'clock had made good progress. Then, when I stopped to eat a bar of chocolate, I was suddenly overwhelmed by the bright stillness around me. The moon was full, there was no wind, and the black silhouette of a church spire was sharp against the sky. I felt moved and happy, and thought I could sense the same emotions even in Fireworks. I know that I consulted her, as if she were a relative or friend en-titled to express her opinion; and I said, in effect:

'What about it, Fireworks? Shall we get away from this hard, silly road, and try the fields?'

I have long forgotten if Fireworks gave any signs of understanding, but a few moments later I had un-latched a gate in the hedge, climbed aboard and set off on a gallop under the moon and stars.

We went straight home across country, jumping gates, stiles, and stone walls all the way, with Fire-works inspired and sensing something significant even if it was not the adolescent glow that ran through *my* frame. I sang, recited poems, and talked to the pony. Then I pretended we were on a midnight steeplechase, and that in turn reminded me of the framed print we had at home, depicting the first of all the steeplechases some hundred and fifty years earlier; and I imagined *we* were there, too, Fireworks and I, leading the 'chase of 1792. Nearing home, I was brought back to earth by a rude grunting from a sleepless pig. But it mat-tered no longer, for Fireworks and I had finished our course, won the race, and jumped our way through history, across the fields, over the gates, under the moon.

Horse of Air

LUCY REES

This is a contemporary story about a girl who meets a horse. I do not find this passage plausible, but it is so well written it carries a splendid conviction. The Welsh cob, Brenin, comes over as a great character and the book describes the heroine's difficulties in coming to terms with him. At the end, penniless, she rides him back to Wales to start a new life. A knowledgeable, unusual story.

> *Ail y carw, olwg gorwyllt,*
> *A'i draed yn gwau drwy dân gwyllt,*
> *A bwrw naid i'r wybr a wnâi,*
> *Ar hyder yr ehedai.*

> Like the deer, his eye frenzied,
> Feet weaving through wild fire,

He loosed a leap at heaven,
Sure of his power to fly.

Asking for the Stallion: Tudur Aled

Quite literally, he bowled me over. When I
looked back over the circumstances in
which I found that horse, the sheer improbability of
it is astounding.

I had been asked to a party (which was pretty
unusual) by Wally and Sally, out of pity, or sense
of duty maybe. What was more unusual was that
I had accepted. It was about thirty miles away, on
a farm where there were horses. We were to stay
the night, so I was sneakily hoping for a ride on
the Sunday. Anyway, it seemed like a minor
adventure.

Saturday evening saw us lost somewhere on the
Kent border, looking for a different family whose
house was 'just on the way' and whom Sally wanted
to see. Sally and Wally argued theatrically, while I
crouched in the back wishing I had not come.
Wally drove too fast and kept missing turnings until we were hopelessly snarled up in tiny lanes,
with Sally totally unable to work out where we
were.

'Give me that map.' Wally lurched to a halt.

'If you didn't drive like a lunatic —' Sally began,
holding it out of his reach.

'If you knew your left from your right . . . Give it

to me, damn it, you stupid cow.' He snatched the map as she flung angrily out of the car and stalked up the lane. After a few moments she came back and knocked on Wally's window.

'Do you know your back tyre's flat?'

Five minutes later, having decided I was superfluous, I was wandering down the dusky lane, smelling the great clumps of cow parsley that hung out from the hedges as the sounds of their bickering died away. Instead there came the drumming of unshod hoofs along the lane, and the next moment a dark, wild-eyed horse careered out of the shadows at me, halter rope swinging. I stood my ground, waving to stop him and, as he crashed into me, lunged for his rope. There are very few horses that will knock you down, and very few that will pull you off your feet; this one did both. I wrapped the rope round my hand as I was dragged along, praying that he would not kick my face in.

Stupidly, I would not let go, and was battered along the lane until we came abruptly to a halt. Shaking like a leaf, I crawled slowly to my feet. The horse looked at me in surprise, nudged me hard with his nose, let out a great bellowing neigh and started to walk purposefully onwards.

There was no way I could stop him: he was just too strong, a powerful fifteen hands of cob with a massive cresty neck. A stallion's neck. His walk grew more urgent, and I realized that he was going to speed up and drag me off my feet again soon. I

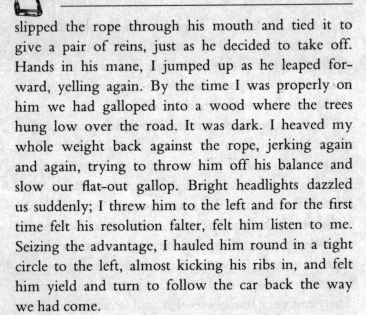

slipped the rope through his mouth and tied it to give a pair of reins, just as he decided to take off. Hands in his mane, I jumped up as he leaped forward, yelling again. By the time I was properly on him we had galloped into a wood where the trees hung low over the road. It was dark. I heaved my whole weight back against the rope, jerking again and again, trying to throw him off his balance and slow our flat-out gallop. Bright headlights dazzled us suddenly; I threw him to the left and for the first time felt his resolution falter, felt him listen to me. Seizing the advantage, I hauled him round in a tight circle to the left, almost kicking his ribs in, and felt him yield and turn to follow the car back the way we had come.

Instantly he was full throttle in that direction, and I realized he just wanted to go anywhere, fast. Roughly, decisively, I drove him from one side of the road to the other: anything to stop him from taking off again. When I felt him get ready to try, I was quick enough and hauled him round in a spin. But I was shaking and exhausted by now. Where on earth were we going? What was I going to do? My pretence of control was feeble, and he would soon cart me off again. Judging by the amount of sweat on him he might have come miles.

I felt weak and, suddenly, for the first time, very frightened.

Wally. Soon I would go back past Wally. Two of us might be able to tie the horse up. Sailor Wally must have ropes, must know how to use them quickly too.

They were standing by the newly changed wheel, and looked amazed, as well they might. I knew I could not stop: instead I yelled.

'Wally, help. Please help. Bring the car and find a rope.'

He stared blankly at me.

'I can't stop,' I roared, level with him now. 'Mad horse. Turn the car, find a rope.'

He leaped in the car as I passed, turned it round behind us, and caught up as we pirouetted in a gateway. 'What next?'

'ROPE, tie him up, I can't stop him.' I could see Sally lean over to the back and start rummaging. The car drew ahead and the horse slowed, following. Wally's head poked out of the window.

'You OK?'

'Yes, better, thanks. Telegraph post, tie him, can't hold him.'

Sally waved a rope at me as Wally shouted, 'Go slow,' and accelerated round the corner. The horse tried to speed up to follow; twice I managed to turn him, but the third time I felt his back coming up under me like a great wave, and knew he was too much. He leaped forward with me tugging unfelt, and as we shot round the corner there was the car slewed across to block the road and Wally, rope in hand, in the gap between it and the hedge. The horse faltered before surging on. I aimed for Wally, felt him catch my rein and check us, felt the horse plunge and rear, and fell off.

But they had done it. Sally had tied one end of the rope to the telegraph post before Wally slipped the other end through my rein. The horse was fighting and screaming, but they had got him, though the rope was too long.

'Do you come here often?' Wally bent over me as I lay bleeding and shaking. My face felt funny.

Sally tied a second rope from the horse to the other side of the road so he could only move a few steps forwards and backwards, and came over.

'Oh, stop it, Wally. Now, let's get you cleaned up.'

'No, I'm OK,' I said, removing a lump of road from the hole in my knee. 'Let's look at him.'

Yes, he was a stallion, a little bull of a horse built like a steam engine on legs, with a massy crest, tiny ears, and a clever little pony face. Huge brown eyes surveyed me carefully, then he reached out his little nose and smelled my face, my ears, my chin, neck, shoulders, arms . . . all the way down to my feet, touching, exploring. Raising his head, he nudged me on the shoulder, turning me round. I felt his breath on the back of my head; he smelled me all the way down to my heels, taking his time. When he had finally finished he blew softly down his nose and waited.

He was my horse.

There are times in your life when there's no doubt at all in your mind, and this was one of them. I had ridden hundreds of horses, liked half of those, fallen in love with maybe five. But this was my horse. My one and only. Everybody has one, but most of us are not lucky enough to find it.

He was dark. I could not see in the gloom, but I thought him dark bay. Sweat made him darker. There was no white on him at all, from his noble forehead to his shaggy heels. He was heavier and smaller than the sort of horse I liked, not my type at all, but there was still no doubt that he was my horse. I put my hand on his steaming shoulder, and it came away dark with blood.

He was cut all over his chest and legs – not very deeply, but as if he had been through a fence. He stood quietly, in the manner of a king humouring his physician, while I felt his legs. But then he started to get restless again, neighing angrily into the dark, pawing and snorting.

'Where do we go from here?' asked Wally. 'It's like having a tiger by the tail.'

Voices came through the dusk and two figures appeared, panting. They were long-haired, bejeaned.

'Wow, man, how d'you get him? Fantastic. Ah, no, really, that was something. Wow. Hey, man, what you doing?' He stroked the horse's neck as the second figure ran back up the lane again. Anyone looking less likely to be involved with horses would be hard to imagine. He wore a headband, beads and sandals, but the Indian effect was dispelled by his emaciation and giggles. He squatted on his heels and rolled a cigarette.

'Wow, what a scene. Thought we'd lost him for good.'

'Is he yours?'

'Well, no, not really, I mean, like he's not mine at all, he belongs to everyone. Except I guess he could be Stevie's. Or was. Is. Was. I don't know.'

Question though I might, I could not work out who did own the horse, nor what had happened. It all seemed like a dream, except for the cold, and the way I ached and shivered. Then some more people drifted up in the dark. More hair; a girl in a long skirt, a fellow holding a bridle as if it were old sea-weed. They were in no hurry, and it was some time before the one with the bridle asked: 'Look, are you sort of really into horses?'

Puzzled by the concept, I nodded.

'Well, do you think you could get him home? 'Cause we can't.'

In the end I rode him back behind a car full of hair. Surprisingly, the bridle they had produced was a double, to which the little horse was evidently well used, and with the curb tight for safety, we trotted powerfully home. I was glad the car was in front.

Off-hand they asked if we would like to stay, and in the end I persuaded Wally and Sally to leave me there; a hard job, but they seemed to understand my reluctance to go to the party. When I went to the loo and saw my face in the mirror I too understood. The right half of it looked like raw steak, while the left half was distorted by two huge lumps and a bloody eye. It was ghastly.

Never mind my face: what about my horse? I went to the barn to see him. In the harsh electric light he looked bigger, and the presence and pride of him were overwhelming in that small space. He was short and powerful, like one of Leonardo's horses. He was also nervy and angry, snapping at me with his ears flat. Yet he had such a lovely eye that I could not believe he was really vicious.

I tied him up and groomed him. His coat was thick with scurf, the sign of an ungroomed stabled horse, and although he was evidently well fed he felt soft. I brushed and slapped and wondered, whistling softly so that he relaxed. I was enormously happy: doing something for a horse like that is a joy and a pleasure, even when you ache all over.

One side was done when Mike, the fellow with the bridle, came and sat in the manger with his girl. And persistently, little by little, I winkled the story out of them.

His name was Brenin something, and he was a Welsh cob – and clearly a good one. He had been brought from Wales years before by a 'hard-faced old cow' in Sussex. She had paid a lot of money for him, although his pedigree was incomplete, for he was 'really well trained'. But the horse disliked her groom: 'Man, he was a maniac, that creep. He had this real hang-up about domination, and he used to beat Brenin up, you know?' But he had at least had some control over the stallion, and when he left it became clear that no one else did. Left with this powerful and by now raging animal, the old cow sold him cheaply to Stevie, a rich Californian who had joined the commune and spent his money freely on livestock. Brenin was bought a mare, and calmed down in her company. But this admirable arrangement did not last long, for Stevie was branded as undesirable and shipped back to the States. 'Sell the horses' were his last instructions. The mare was sold the night their advertisement appeared in the paper, but not so Brenin, who went wild without her. And the more difficult he got, the more he had to be shut up, which made him worse. He had spent five months in the stable, with even the door and the window barred, slowly going mad. That afternoon they had made one last attempt at taking him out, but there was no way they could hold him – as I had discovered. By now he was too tense, too crazy, too strong. Who would want a horse like that?

I stroked his broad buttock. 'How much do you want for him?'

'Five hundred, supposed to be.'

I went back to brushing.

But even if I could not have him I could try to give him a better deal. I wondered if they would let me stay for the weekends; they did not seem to be bothered by anything very much. The house was big, rambling, casual and dirty; it could have done with a cleaner. There were quite a few of them, and they were a bit strange, given to smiling silently and stroking each other, but they were not frightening. They did not want to peer and pry at me.

They gave me herbal tea made of eyebright and honey, which was odd but delicious, in a kitchen full of rough wooden tables and implements, glass and crockery, jars of beans and seeds, and a profusion of vegetables piled in one corner. Green and burnt earth colours in a multitude of textures. Curiously, it was oil paint I hankered for, rather than the more usual pencil or charcoal.

In the morning I seemed to spin, completely disorientated. Some mornings you wake up confused because you don't know which way your feet are pointing. This time it was towards a battered harp, two sheepskins, an odd smell and a reproduction of an Indian sculpture of a coy, curvy girl with smiling almond eyes and round round breasts.

Brenin seemed smaller and friendlier at first, but then he grew restless, knocking me over quite deliberately.

'That's what happens when you try to lead him,' said Mike, appearing over the top of the door. 'You can't hold on to him.'

'It seems such a shame. If he's shut up now he'll

only brood about yesterday. If I put that bridle on him I could hold him if I rode him . . .'

He came crashing out of the box so fast I nearly lost my footing, but after a few steps he stopped rigid to throw up his head and bellow out a challenge to the world. Mike threw me up and we hurtled into the paddock.

Riding stallions is quite different from riding mares or geldings, for their necks and shoulders are so heavy and massy that you feel quite safe – at least in terms of falling off. Brenin got his hind legs up under him in a most uncoblike way, so that with his great crest in front it felt as if he were about to rise slowly from the ground. He pulled me round the paddock several times before I dared suggest what to do. And then I had the best ride of my life. He was not the best-schooled horse I had ever ridden, nor fast; but for half an hour I was completely absorbed in trying to come up to his standard, to be a worthy companion to his hot-headed little self. He went puffing and snorting round as if he were listening for the clash of battle-arms, looking for the captains and the shouting. He was as fearless and proud as that horse of Job's, his neck clothed with thunder.

But I could not get him to relax, and my arms felt as if they might come out of their sockets, so I had to take him back in. It was only then that I realized that the whole commune had turned out to watch. I was staggering into the box with him when a girl ran up and kissed me on the cheek.

'That was so beautiful,' she said in an American accent. 'You and that horse, it was just incredible.'

I did not know what to say. He was my horse – or I was his person. And both of us knew it.

Another Pony for Jean

JOANNA CANNAN

Hunting, which many people are currently against, is a part of the horse world: show-hunters, hunter trials, point-to-points, even the Grand National are all based on the sport. Many today conveniently forget about other methods of killing foxes: think of it, the cruelty involved in putting poison gas into an earth with cubs in it, of shooting and perhaps only wounding, of snaring, the worst cruelty of all, perfectly legal and still common – are these less cruel than hunting? Less cruel than killing rats with Warfarin (a dreadful death), moles with cyanide, and destroying thousands of pet dogs every year? The only person out hunting concerned with killing the fox is the huntsman, controlling his hounds. All the others are only followers, far more worried about whether they will survive the next fence than whether the fox gets caught. As this piece shows.

The morning was fine but rather windy. I had allowed an hour and a half to get to Coney Farm, but Cavalier was fresh and along most of the road there was a wide grass edge where we could canter, so we arrived rather early. I walked Cavalier up and down to prevent him getting cold and we watched the people arriving. My deceiving pilot arrived in a huge car; a groom had brought his chestnut. Another very smart person was a girl of about twenty who came in a car with the Master. She wore a top hat, and a bunch of violets in her buttonhole. She had a fashionable face and lots of rolled-up curls the shape of sausages. Her name seemed to be Pamela.

Well, after a bit hounds arrived and presently we moved off towards a wood which I had noticed on the map; it has rather a lovely name – Hangman's Hollow. There wasn't a very large field and I managed to recognize Colonel Craven, whom my cousins had told me generally acted as Field Master. When the huntsman put the hounds into Hangman's Hollow I stayed with the Field Master, which is much better than trying to be knowing and not succeeding.

We found in Hangman's Hollow. The fox went away from the other side of the wood and we all went charging through it. Cavalier was very clever at threading his way through the trees; it reminded me of a bending race. There was a messy little jump out of the wood into a field and we galloped across the field, which was pasture, and jumped a nice tidy hedge and galloped on again. It was lovely because the ground was rising a bit and you could see the whole pack in full cry; I must say it looked awfully like a Christmas card or a calendar. We had two more jumps over nice hedges and then we came to a nasty place. There was a huge overgrown hedge that the farmer had been too lazy to layer; it was about nine feet high and all messed up with brambles, and the only place where you could possibly jump it was in a corner where the hedge didn't grow properly because of a tree. To strengthen the gap the farmer had put up two bars made out of sawn-off branches, and they were wired to a sharp stake. You couldn't jump to the right of the stake because of an overhanging branch of the tree, but you could jump to the left of the stake if you didn't mind scratching yourself on sticking-out bits of the hedge and trailing brambles.

Well, we got to the gap and people had to go over one by one. Cavalier was rather impatient; he danced about like a rocking-horse. At last everybody was over except me and the fashionable girl called Pamela and two people on rather thin horses, who couldn't make up their minds whether to jump or not. If you have hunted much, I expect you have met people like them – the man said to the woman, 'Are you going to jump this, Maud?' And Maud, instead of saying yes or no, said, 'Well, I don't know, Edward. What do *you* think?' Edward said, 'It looks nasty but everybody seems to be jumping it. I don't really mind.'

And Maud said, 'I don't mind either.' And Edward said, 'Well, dear, just as you think.' Some people, who didn't like the look of the jump or knew their horses couldn't jump it, had gone back through the field and through a gate and round; Maud and Edward might just as well have done that as stand dithering all this time. However, Maud suddenly made up her mind to jump. She put her horse at the jump in a very uncertain way and of course he refused, and then, instead of getting out of the way and letting someone else have a chance, she tried again. She tried about ten times and then she said she thought it would be best to go round.

Edward said he thought so too, and they turned their thin horses round and cantered away. Then Pamela put her lovely grey hunter at the jump and something happened which was going to make a lot of difference to me.

At the time I wasn't expecting anything to happen and I didn't notice exactly what Pamela did, but since then I have thought it over, and I think that what really happened was that Pamela didn't want to be scratched by the sticking-out bits of hedge and the trailing brambles, so, instead of letting her horse jump to the left of the stake, she pulled him over just when he was taking off, and he wasn't expecting to have to jump high enough to clear the stake. Anyhow, the next thing that I saw was an awful muddle. Pamela and the grey were both rolling on the ground, but fortunately they rolled in different directions. Pamela got up almost at once, but the grey lay still for a moment or two. Then he got up in a struggling hurt sort of way, and I saw that blood was spurting from an awful gash in his off foreleg.

For a moment Cavalier and I stood rooted to the ground. Then I realized that, as everybody else had disappeared over the next hedge by now, I was the only person there except Pamela. I put Cavalier at the jump and he hopped neatly over. Pamela was looking rather funny, so I said, 'Are you all right?' and she said, 'Yes, but look at that,' and pointed to the grey.

I got off and went up to him. Blood was absolutely pouring from his wound. I stood rooted to the ground for a moment and then, though I don't usually remember things at a time when they would be of any use, but only in bed hours afterwards, I remembered what Mummy had told me about arteries and tourniquets one day at tea. She had told me how blood runs down your arteries from your heart and how, if a person gets an artery cut, you must bind them up very tight *above* the wound, and we had pretended that one of the dining-room chairs had cut its artery and we had made a bandage of my handkerchief and bound it round the leg of the chair. Then Mummy had told me that probably the bandage wouldn't be tight enough and we must make a tourniquet, so we had got the poker and pushed it through the bandage and turned it round and round until the bandage was frightfully tight and we had saved the life of the chair. I thought of that now, but I knew my handkerchief, which was Mrs Beazley's one with the vicious black horse on it, would be much too small. Then I thought of my hunting tie, so I took off my gloves and undid the pin and nearly strangled myself tugging off the tie. However, I got it off and wound it round the grey's leg and tied it as tight as I could, but still he bled like anything. So I yelled to Pamela, 'Bring a stick!' She said, 'What kind of stick?' But just then I saw my hunting crop lying on the ground with my gloves and pin. I shoved it through the bandage and turned it round and round, and suddenly the bleeding stopped. I *was* pleased.

But I was only pleased for a minute. Then I realized that I had never asked Mummy how to *fasten* a tourniquet, and I knew that if the grey took it into his head to move off or to jump about, I should be done. I *yelled* to Pamela, who was pottering in the hedge – I suppose she was still looking for a stick – and she came, and I said, 'Do you know how to fasten a tourniquet?'

Pamela said, 'No, I don't.' She looked at the grey, and said, 'Ugh! I can't stand the sight of blood. I think I'm going to faint.' And she turned away.

I expect you will think I was very silly and babyish, but honestly I couldn't think *what* to do. I stood holding the tourniquet and looking helplessly round, and then suddenly I saw a sight that gladdened my eyes. It was hats bobbing about over the hedge in the next field. I shrieked at Pamela, 'Take my pony and go and fetch someone.' And then I remembered that I had let go of Cavalier. I couldn't turn right round, but I screwed my head round as far as it would go and out of the corner of my eye I could see him quietly grazing under the tree. Pamela went up to him and luckily he stood still. Then nothing happened for ages so I yelled at her, 'Aren't you going?' She said, 'I'm letting the stirrups down.'

I'm afraid I was very rude. I forgot that she was grown-up. I said, 'Oh, gosh, you *are* feeble!' Pamela said, 'There's no need to be rude,' and trotted cautiously off across the field.

After what seemed to be ages, she got to the hedge. I suppose she shouted over it; anyhow, a bobbing hat came up to the hedge and then another, and then one of the whippers-in and a man on a big bay thoroughbred came over.

They galloped across the field, but before they came right up to me they dismounted and the whipper-in held the horses, and the other man came running. He said to me, 'That's all right – I'm a veterinary surgeon.' And he knelt down and took hold of my tourniquet. Then several other people arrived – so I got out of their way and went off and looked for Cavalier. Pamela still had him up by the hedge where she was talking to someone.

I walked across the field and I must own up that my legs felt wobbly – I do wish that I was one of those people who remain calm and unruffled in emergencies. However, I got across the field all right and when Pamela saw me, she said, 'Well, what happened?'

I said, 'A vet is seeing to your horse. Can I have my pony, please?'

Pamela said, 'Oh, certainly,' and dismounted. Then she said to the other person, 'Goodness knows how I'm going to get home. I'd better find Uncle George.'

She walked off to find Uncle George. I found a low place in the hedge and Cavalier hopped over. I must own up that I held on to his mane because my silly legs still felt wobbly.

The field I had jumped into was a very rough field, full of hounds and bushes. Hounds had checked there, which had been lucky for me – if they had run straight on, goodness knows what would have happened. Everyone was standing still while the huntsman made his cast, so, as I was now feeling very hungry, I ate my sandwiches. I had eaten two when I heard a hound speaking and hastily crammed the others back into my pocket. Then we were off again, galloping over the rough field and yelling, ''Ware hole!' at each other.

It was a very short run. We soon came to a wood and there I think the fox went to ground. Anyhow, we waited about for ages and then, owing to my hands being cold, I suddenly remembered that I had left my gloves, tie-pin and hunting crop at the place where the grey had staked himself. I thought that I had better collect them or I should never find the place again, so I turned reluctantly round, said, 'Good night!' to one or two people, who had said things like 'What a nice pony!' or 'Do you like hunting?' to me, and set off down the hill and through the rough field. Cavalier jumped the hedge very neatly, and when we were over I saw a horse-box just going out of the field. I realized that it was taking the grey horse home, and I wondered where his home was.

I rode to the fatal spot but I couldn't find any of my things. I felt very sorrowful at first, and then it occurred to me that some obliging person had collected them and would probably send them back to me. So I followed the tracks of the horse-box and soon I found myself in a lane. I rode along it in what I thought was the right direction and presently I came to a road and a helpful signpost, which said 'Long Crickenden'. After about five miles of that road I came out on Crickenden Heath and then of course I turned right and was soon at Hedgers Green.

Mummy was very pleased that I had come home before she got nervous. As we rugged up Cavalier I told her about the grey and how idiotic I had been about fastening the tourniquet. Mummy said she didn't think I had been fearfully idiotic considering my age, and when I told Daddy about it he said that I had behaved with courage and dispatch, so I felt quite pleased.

That night I dreamed about Pamela. I dreamed that I scrambled some eggs for her and took an awful lot of trouble over them, but when they were finished she said that they were all wrong. I can't *think* why I was scrambling eggs for her. I do have silly dreams.

★

I was rather late for breakfast next morning. When I got down to the dining-room there was a letter on my plate. It was in a thick square bluish envelope – not like bills – and on the back of the envelope was a crest. It was some weird sort of bird and there was a Latin motto under it, which I was not far on enough in Latin to translate. I thought the letter must be from some girl at school whom I didn't like – it is nearly always girls you don't like who write to you in the holidays. I poured out my milk and opened my letter.

It began *My dear Miss Jean*, which was funny, so I looked at the end. It was signed *Your grateful servant, Highmoor*.

I couldn't *think* who it was from, so I read it through. Gradually I realized that it was from Lord Highmoor thanking me politely for having saved the life of the grey horse, on which he had mounted his niece from London, and asking me to give him the pleasure of my company at tea at Highmoor Court at four o'clock tomorrow. I *was* surprised. I said, 'Gosh, look at this,' and gave Mummy the letter.

Mummy said she wished I wouldn't say gosh and read the letter. She said that it was very nice and that I had better go.

I said that I thought she ought to go because it was really she who had saved the grey's life by telling me sensible things about arteries instead of idiotic things about fairies. Mummy said, 'Nonsense,' and she said that if I went, Lord Highmoor would probably show me his stables. So then I said I would go.

After breakfast Mummy made me write a polite note. It said that I would love to come to tea at four o'clock tomorrow and that I had been glad to be able to help with the grey. I signed it like Lord Highmoor had signed his – *your grateful servant*, but Mummy said that I ought to have put *yours sincerely*. However, owing to blots and spelling mistakes I had already copied the beastly thing out three times, so I said that I really couldn't do it again.

Cavalier was having a rest after hunting, so later on in the morning I walked up to Highmoor Court and took the dogs. In the drive a red and white sports car passed me. Pamela and luggage were inside.

The next day was wet. I drew horses and hunting scenes in the morning and in the first part of the afternoon I took Shadow and Sally for a short, wet walk. I went without a hat and my hair got lovely and wet. When I arrived home Mummy shrieked and said where on earth had I been and look at my hair; it would never be dry, she said, in time for me to go to Highmoor Court. I rushed upstairs and dried my hair, and changed into riding clothes in case Lord Highmoor should offer me a ride on a thoroughbred.

When I went downstairs Mummy said that I ought to have put on my Fair Isle sweater and grey flannel skirt and that I still looked like a drowned rat. It was too late to change again – in fact, as Daddy had the car and I had got to walk, it was time for me to start, but Mummy insisted on getting a bath towel and drying my head. I was filled with impatience and couldn't help jumping up and down and saying, 'What does hair matter?' And after a bit Mummy said it was the best she could do, so she let me go and I rushed off.

The rain had stopped so I didn't bother about a hat, but, as I was going through the village, it started to pour – absolute cats and dogs. I couldn't take shelter because of being late, so I walked on, but before I came in sight of Highmoor Court I stopped and dried my face on my handkerchief and wrung out my hair.

Highmoor Court is a stately home of England. There are deer in the park, cedars on the lawn and a fountain on the terrace and stone lions and things. The front door is at the side. I walked up to it and rang the bell.

The bell was answered by Clarence Funge, who is a footman. I know his mother, so I asked after her as I politely wiped my feet on the mat. Clarence said that she was suffering awful from her legs. I said I was sorry to hear it and I hoped that she would soon be all right.

Clarence took me into a huge sort of hall. There were family portraits all round it and exciting weapons – lovely battle-axes for hacking people to pieces with and rapiers suitable for duels at dawn. At the far end of the hall there was a lordly tea-table spread with shining silver and lots of buns, and in front of the huge log fire stood Lord Highmoor with two Clumber spaniels, a dog and a bitch.

I walked across the hall towards Lord Highmoor

and he walked across the hall towards me. It took ages, but at last we met in the middle. We shook hands and said, 'How-do-you-do?' Then neither of us could think of anything to say.

There was an awful silence until suddenly I noticed that my hair was dripping. So I said politely, 'Excuse my hair.'

Lord Highmoor said by jove, I did look rather wet, and he suggested that I should come nearer the fire. He got a cushion for me and I knelt on it with my hair over my face. Lord Highmoor suggested that he should go out to the stable and fetch a straw wisp and a curry comb and we got the giggles, and he said that I looked like a Dartmoor pony, and I said that *he* looked like a reliable cob with a hogged mane and mouth and manners, so we weren't nearly as polite as I had expected we should be.

When my hair was dry, we had tea. There were enough buns for a school treat and some pink iced cakes, which I had to eat as the cook had made them specially for me. We talked about Cavalier and then we talked about the grey. We did get rather polite then because Lord Highmoor *would* thank me again and all I could think of saying was, 'Please don't mention it,' and 'Not at all.' We went on like that for a bit and then Lord Highmoor said that, as the grey was one of his favourite horses and very valuable, he would like to make me a small present. I said, 'Oh, no, you mustn't,' but he said he would be most upset and miserable if I didn't take it, so I said, all right, I would. I wondered what on earth the present would be.

It sounded most mysterious. He said it was something he had bought for his nephew, who was Pamela's younger brother and his heir, but the nephew was nervous and didn't like it. Then he sighed and looked sad, and I said it must be awful to have a nervous heir.

Lord Highmoor said it was, and that if I had had enough to eat we would go out and look at the present. I said that I had heaps, and pulled out my handkerchief to remove crumbs. Of course masses of oats and some lumps of sugar leaped out of my pocket with my handkerchief and strewed themselves about the floor. I stood rooted to the ground, but Lord Highmoor said that it was an improvement. He said that the room had looked much too tidy before.

We went out by a door at the end of the hall. The rain had stopped, so we walked along the terrace and I turned the fountain on and off and rode the stone lions. Then we went through a door in a wall, and I found myself in a lovely stable-yard with a clock tower and white fantail pigeons flying about, and all the lovely heads of the hunters looking over the tops of the doors.

Lord Highmoor's horses were nearly all called by the names of virtues. There was Truth and Prudence and Hope. Truth and Prudence were big brown geldings and Hope was a lovely chestnut mare. Then there was Patience, who was a grey mare, and there was a roan cob, which Lord Highmoor used for hacking — her name was Faith. There was a very old hunter called Justice; he was really too old to hunt, but Lord Highmoor took him out cubbing sometimes because he loved hunting so. And then there was the old dog-cart horse, whose name was Judge. He was twenty-five and occasionally Lord Highmoor drove him in a light dog-cart, not long distances but just round the farms.

I talked to all the horses and forgot about my present, but after a bit Lord Highmoor said I *must* come on. We went to the side of the yard where the clock tower was, and I thought that perhaps he was going to take me into the harness room and give me a martingale or something, but we passed the harness room and went to a loose box in the corner that I hadn't noticed. It was the same sort of loose box that the hunters had, with the same sort of door, and looking over the top of it was a little grey head belonging to someone quite small. I went and looked over and there was a lovely little cob, almost milk white, with a hogged mane and a long tail.

Lord Highmoor said, 'This is the pony I bought for my nephew. I do hope you'll have her. Her name is Charity.'

Words failed me. I stood rooted to the ground. Lord Highmoor said, 'She's twelve two, so she'll fit you all right now, and she's only rising five, so when you grow out of her you'll be able to use her as a little brood mare.'

I still couldn't think of anything to say. Then at last I managed to gasp out, 'But doesn't your nephew want her?' It was an idiotic remark because I had already been told that the nephew was nervous, but if you like riding yourself, it is hard to believe that there actually are children who don't.

Lord Highmoor said, 'I'm afraid he doesn't. He likes bicycles and model trains.'

'How awful,' I said.

'Well, everybody can't like the same thing,' said Lord Highmoor, being broad-minded, which Mummy always says I ought to be. 'It would be a dull world if they did. I wouldn't mind at all, only it's rather saddening to think that one day there'll be no horses in these boxes and no hounds up at Boveney Hatch.'

Boveney Hatch is where the kennels are. It is on Lord Highmoor's estate about three miles beyond Long Crickenden.

I said, 'Perhaps your nephew will reform,' and then I looked at Charity, and I said, 'She *is* lovely, but I'm sure this is only a dream.'

Lord Highmoor pinched me to show that it wasn't, and then he asked if my parents would mind having another pony. I said I was sure they wouldn't because we were now richer and could afford hay.

It was now dark. Lord Highmoor had turned on the light in Charity's box and the grooms, who were getting busy with pitchforks and buckets, had turned on a light under the clock tower. Lord Highmoor said that I had better not take Charity tonight as it was dark, but he would send a groom over with her the next day.

I said, 'All right.' And then I suddenly realized that this lovely little white cob was really going to be mine. I realized that she was actually going to walk up the drive to our stable, and live there and in the orchard, and that I should have two hunters and two ponies to ride in gymkhanas. I said, 'Oh, thank you, thank you, thank you frightfully.' And Lord Highmoor said that it was only a small return for what I had done for his grey.

We were still being polite when a groom appeared with a feed for Charity. It was beginning to rain again and Lord Highmoor said should he send me home in his car? I said, 'No, thank you. I like getting wet,' and we went back to the house. Half-way across the stable-yard I glanced back and there was Charity still looking over her door. The light was on in her box and she was just like a white angel horse looking out of heaven. I made Lord Highmoor look and he thought so too.

There was lemonade with ice in it waiting for me on a table in the hall. I drank it and said I really must be going, and of course I said thank you for everything again.

Then I went, because it is irritating when people stay for ages after they have said that they must go. I cantered down the drive and jogged through Hedgers Green and trotted a bit and then galloped the rest of the way home. I refused the gate so my rider, who was rather nervous, opened it, and I tore in.

Mummy was sitting in the drawing-room reading. She said, 'Hullo!'

I said, 'Hullo!' I was too much out of breath to say anything more for a minute, but after a bit, between gasps, I told her.

My parents are strict about some things. They are awfully strict about being rude or wanting things you can't have or grumbling or saying 'Bother' when they ask you to fetch them things, but in many ways they are most obliging. Some parents would have said that I didn't need another pony or that it would only be another expense for them, but Mummy said, 'How lovely,' and when Daddy came in, he said he didn't mind how many ponies I had, but he did wish that I'd do something about my hair.

Who, Sir? Me, Sir?

K. M. PEYTON

Nails was generally asleep not long after ten, preferring to get up when the sun did, take Firelight out and clean up her stable and do his running practice before going home for breakfast. Firelight generally ate a bit of her haynet and by the time he settled down to go to sleep she lay down as well.

But this night the mare was restless. She kept walking round her box, sighing, and picking bits out of her haynet and dropping them on the floor. While Nails was still reading his comic, she lay down and got up twice, which had never happened before. Nails put down his comic and looked at her closely, worried.

'What's wrong with you?'

His complete ignorance regarding horses, except how to ride them, came home to him as he sensed there was something wrong. He got up, worried.

Firelight came up and licked his outstretched hand, snorted sharply and tossed her head. Then she kicked up at her belly with one hind-leg and sighed gustily again. Or was it a groan? Nails became miserable with anxiety. He half-thought of going to Nutty's house, but it was getting late. She would be in bed by now, like as not. Her mother would be cross and he would feel stupid.

He thought Firelight was ill. Something was worrying her. How could you tell if a horse had a pain? They did not go pale, or frown, or faint. He put down the comics and sat watching her. But then she fell to eating her haynet as usual, so he decided she had a touch of indigestion, and it had passed. He fetched his sleeping-bag from the corn bin, where he kept it so the mice wouldn't make a nest in it, and curled up to go to sleep. He dozed off with the familiar, soothing noise of Firelight's hay-chomping over his head.

He was woken some time later by being kicked in the backside quite painfully. He sat up indignantly. In the darkness he could see that Firelight was lying down, but there was nothing unusual in that. But she was breathing very heavily and jerking her legs in a funny way, as if something hurt her. He stared, frightened, and she lay very quiet, as if kidding him. It was too dark to see her expression, whether it was sleepy or distressed. He scrambled out of his sleeping-bag and went to fetch a torch he kept for when he wanted to read late, not liking to put on the light and get all the others going. They always thought it was feed time if the light went on and would scramble up expectantly and start pawing and whinnying. He came back with the torch and shone it on her. She looked at him, blinking. She looked quite as usual. He let the torch travel down over her back, to take her all in, and was surprised to see something peculiar under her tail. There was something sticking out.

Nails felt his stomach contract in a peculiar way. He felt both repelled and terrified. There was something definitely wrong, but what it was he had no idea. He thought she had a growth, or was losing her innards in some revolting way. Past visions of run-over cats and spilt intestines made his skin prick with horror. The mare's breathing was heavy and distressed and she kept turning her head round to him as if asking him for help.

'Gawd, what's wrong with you?' he muttered, feeling quite helpless, and terribly frightened.

It was pitch-dark and felt like the small hours; there was no sound of traffic from the road at all, and he was on his own with a vengeance. The other horses were asleep.

'Firelight! Be all right! You're not going to die, are you?'

There was no one to hear his pathetic funk; it really didn't matter what he said. The mare gave a sigh and a great shudder ran through her. She struggled a bit in the straw, and the growth under her tail seemed to grow suddenly while he shone his torch on it. His hand trembled. The growth was a sort of shiny, membrane-covered thing. Nails watched it with horrified fascination, and saw it start to slide towards him. The membrane broke open and he found himself looking at a little horse's head lying upon a pair of stretched-out forelegs, a perfect little head with shell-like curling nostrils and a narrow white blaze, and wet, flattened-down ears. While he held this vision in the trembling torchlight, the eyes opened and looked at him, reflecting back the light of his torch. He was shocked rigid; even his breathing stopped. He actually felt his mouth fall open with the shock. And while he watched, Firelight gave a great heave and a whole lot more of the little horse slid out, its neck and mane and withers and then its whole backside complete with tail, spilt out in a heap in the straw, ungainly legs in a pale tangle.

Nails stared. For a moment he thought he was going to pass out. Although he now realized what the phenomenon was that he had just witnessed, he found it impossible to digest the truth before his very eyes: Firelight had given birth to a baby. Firelight hadn't been expecting a baby! Even Biddy, who knew everything, had never suggested such a thing was going to happen, and certainly Mr Bean nor Nutty had never said anything. Nutty had once accused him of giving his mare extra feed at night because she was fatter than all the others, but it was true: he did give her extra. She was fatter. She had been fat with a baby. Nails found his shock giving way to the shakes and the shakes to an immense compulsion to laugh. The little horse was the most extraordinary thing that had ever happened to him in all his life, appearing like that in the torchlight and looking at him even before it was wholly born, as if to say, 'Hi, mate.' It was now thrashing feebly about in the straw trying to get its tangle of legs in order, a whole, complete, new horse – when five minutes ago there had been nothing at all save him thinking Firelight had indigestion.

Nails laughed then. He squatted down in the straw looking at the foal, and the foal looked back at him, indignant, bright-eyed, quivering with life. Life! He had seen it happen, like a click of the fingers, the start of life, when the foal opened its eyes and looked at him. It was almost too much to take in, how it had happened so quickly, so unexpectedly. Nails was laughing and shivering at the same time, so excited that he felt almost ill with it. He was as trembly and thrown out as the foal.

'You little fellow, you . . . you lovely baby,' he warbled idiotically. He had no idea whether it was a male or a female. He never really had noticed things like that about horses. He remembered that Firelight had to feed it with milk, but where she kept it he had no idea. As she got to her feet he looked underneath her, remembering the equipment cows had, and saw that she had a semblance of the same thing, although nothing like so dangly as a cow's, but quite satisfactorily dripping at that moment with what he supposed was milk. She stood over the foal licking it and nuzzling it and licking it again. There was the slimy membrane and some messy stuff that Nails cleared away diligently and threw outside; he got some fresh straw and by the time he had done that the foal was trying to stand up, with great difficulty. It could not control its folding legs, and Nails helped it, holding its backside up while it propped up its front end. All the time he had this great bursting feeling of utter incredulity inside him; it kept exploding, he kept laughing out loud at the memory of the amazing appearance before his very eyes of this whole new life; the shock of it would not fade.

By the time the foal had tottered and swayed and nuzzled at Firelight in all the wrong places and eventually found the right spot to have a slurp of milk, Nails was surprised to see that it was beginning to go light. He had lost all sense of time and place. It got light at about half-past four, he thought. The foal was lying down again and looking sleepy, and Firelight was dozing over it perfectly contented, and Nails decided to go down and tell Nutty what had happened. There was no point in trying to go to sleep again. He knew he never would.

He went outside, shutting the large doors silently and started off down the concrete road. He was in a dream, aware of the sharp, early air and the smell of damp earth, seeing the vast pearly spread of the estuary far away below him beyond the fading gold necklaces of the street-lights, and yet altogether apart from his everyday world. So far removed from normal sense that when he rang the bell at Nutty's house and her father came down in his dressing-gown thinking it must be the police, he did not understand the excitement.

'It's a quarter to five! Have you gone mad?'

'I want to tell Nutty something.'

'It's not the sort of time that people generally call –'

'It's not the sort of thing that generally happens.'

'Have you been up all night?'

'No. Perhaps.'

Mr McTavish, studying Nails closely, thought the boy was ill and took him into the kitchen and made him a cup of tea. He had never seen Nails before as other than a surly, rude boy, but now he was smiling and looked light-headed.

'You drink this and I'll tell her you're here.'

Nutty came down, blinking, wary.

'Are you all right, Nails? Dad says –'

'Firelight's had a foal.'

Nutty blinked again, frowned.

'You're joking?'

'No. I watched it come out. I *watched* it. You go and look. It's there now. It's lying there in the straw.'

Nutty was bewildered. Nails looked so strange she thought he was off his rocker.

'But you were riding her – yesterday. Nobody said – she –'

'If you don't believe me, go and look.'

But Nutty believed him, and the consequences of the turn of events gradually came home to her, and her face, instead of lighting up with joy, dropped with dismay.

'She can't!' she wailed. 'Not now! Not for the competition! Whatever shall we do?'

'Why?'

'You'll have nothing to ride!'

Nails did not follow, nor care at all. But Nutty, the disaster plain, was almost in tears of consternation. Her father poured out another cup of tea.

'For Gawd's sake, can't we wait till after breakfast? What a way to start the day!'

Nutty had to ring up Biddy straight away – ('Oh, well, it's getting late, it's five o'clock,' her father said. 'I daresay she's been up since three, being horsey.') Biddy, it seemed, was as horrified as Nutty.

'Come and see it,' Nails said.

'Whatever are we going to do?' Nutty kept saying.

She came with him, pulling on her anorak. They ran side by side, easy with training, breathless only with amazement, and now the sun was coming up over the edge of the sea and the whole world was sharp and glittery, concrete and weeds, and the barbed wire hanging drops of dew and spiders' webs. Nails felt as if he was bursting.

'Look at it! Just look at it!' He pulled open the doors of the factory.

Nutty looked, was struck speechless.

The others came up.

'What is it? What's happened?'

'That's happened,' Nails said proudly.

They were all late for school. Nails sat all day in a

trance and every teacher who took his class reported his state to his form-master. Opinion was divided as to whether he was ill or stoned. He had to report to the headmaster at four o'clock, and was taken there by force by Foggerty who caught him racing for the school gates when the bell went.

'I've got something to do!'

'Yes, you have, lad, get to see the head, that's what you've got to do.'

'I haven't done anything wrong!'

'Just look at you, Nicholson. You haven't done anything wrong, perhaps, but have you ever done anything right? You leave school in a few weeks and you've got to make yourself a living. Have you ever thought what sort of a picture you'll make coming up before a prospective employer? Have you seen yourself in a mirror lately?'

Nails had to admit that it was true he slept in his clothes every night; he had bits of straw all over him and probably smelled a bit. He never washed, but considered swimming nearly every day took care of that. He had had nothing to eat that day at all and had been up quite a lot of the night and now felt a bit dozy, but it didn't mean that he was ill.

'There's nothing wrong with me!' he cried out in response to the head's question.

'Are you sure?' the head asked solicitously. 'Anything wrong at home? You know we can help you if you have – er – problems. The staff say you always look as if you've been sleeping in haystacks these days. Is your mother – er – back yet?'

'No, but that doesn't make any difference. She's been gone two years and you never asked before.'

'No, we have been remiss. I wonder if your father would like to come and have a chat with me, possibly about your future? He never put in an appearance at the parents' meeting. I would like to see him.'

Nails shrugged, thinking it highly unlikely. The head put a few notes on a pad and Nails was set free, leaving his teachers puzzled.

And while they were shaking their heads over the modern young in the staff-room, Nutty and her team were congregating at the refrigerator factory to take another look at the amazing happening. It was standing up, bold as brass, its long, stilty legs firmly planted, its ears pricked up, eyes bright, not frightened at all. They hung over the refrigerators, training forgotten.

'What you going to call it, Nails?'

'What is it, a boy or a girl?'

'What is it, Nutty?'

'It's a colt, a boy, stupid. It's got a thing, can't you see?'

'Where?'

'Where d'you think? Same place as yours. You are *stupid*.'

'I never noticed.' Hoomey went to look at Bones, thoughtfully. 'What's Nails going to ride in the competition then? You can't ride a nursing mother.'

Nutty groaned. 'It's ruined everything! Biddy said

she'd come up here tonight. Perhaps she'll have an idea.'

Biddy came up with Uncle Knacker. They stood gazing at the foal, shaking their heads.

'They can still pull a fast one on you,' Biddy admitted. 'Not a sign beforehand. I didn't even think she was fat.'

'And she was going so well! It's a damned shame for the boy. I'll bring the lorry up in the morning and take her away.'

'Take her away where?' Nails whispered.

'She can't stay here, boy. Mare and foal's got to have a field of grass.'

'Where?'

'She'll have to go down in the fattening fields with the cows.'

Nutty looked at Nails and thought for one awful moment he was going to burst into tears. He was as white as a sheet.

'You can't take her away.'

Mr Bean looked at him closely. 'She's got to go, lad. They've got to have a bit of room to move, like.' He considered, still looking at Nails. 'Tell you what. I've got the use of a little field out by the Town Dairy. Old Carter's place. It's only ten minutes out of town. I could put her there if you like. You'd be able to visit there.'

Nails did not reply, but the pinched white look went out of his face. He shrugged, kicked the refrigerator.

'What are we going to do for a horse for you?' Biddy said to him, kindly for her. 'It's put us in a fix.'

'I don't care,' he said.

'Don't you?'

Nails shrugged again.

'Point is, you've got to care, haven't you? That's what a team is all about. Not just for yourself, you've got to do it for the rest. If it's just for yourself and you fall off and hurt yourself you can pull out, and nobody's the worse off, but if you're in a team you've got to get round else the whole team is in the cart. You've ruined it for everyone. So whether you don't care or not, you've still got to do it, haven't you? However much you don't want to.'

Nails scowled. 'All right. I played in the polo team, didn't I? They half-killed you sometimes. You don't have to tell me.'

Biddy was surprised. 'Polo?'

'Him and the Prince of Wales,' Jazz said.

'Water-polo, he means,' Nutty said helpfully.

'Oh.' Biddy laughed. 'Well then. You know. How long is it to the competition?' She appealed to Nutty.

'It's two weeks on Saturday. Seb says we're entered – he put us down. There are about ten other teams, but it's only them we've got to beat.'

'Why not beat the others too while you're about it? In for a penny, in for a pound,' Mr Bean asked.

'We'll concentrate on Greycoats first.'

'You come up to my place tomorrow night, Nails,' Biddy said. 'I shall expect you.'

Nails did not know where it was. Biddy told him. 'In fact,' she added, 'I'll come and fetch you on my motor-bike. I'll pick you up outside school at four.'

'And I'll go and fetch the lorry and take this little mare up to Carter's now,' Uncle Knacker decided.

The adults, with the exception of Uncle Knacker, departed.

'What you going to call it, Nails?' Hoomey started again. 'You got to give it a name. Something like Surprise.'

'Dawn Surprise,' Nutty said.

'Sounds like a pudding,' Jazz said.

'Night Arrival. Midnight Express,' Hoomey said. 'That's a good one. You said it came out really fast. You –'

'Oh, shut up,' Nails said witheringly. 'You're useless at names. What about *Bones*?'

Hoomey looked hurt. 'He probably had a smart name once. I wish I knew what it was. Bones doesn't suit him any more.'

'Should think not, the amount of feed he gets through,' Uncle Knacker said. 'Never seen a doer like it. I'm off to get the lorry then. You can come if you like, Nails, as I suppose we can call you the owner of this new arrival. You want to see it safe in its new quarters.'

Nails saw Firelight duly let out into Carter's field with her foal. The field was not large, but it was full of good grass and had high sheltering hedges of hawthorn round it. On the town side of it, downhill, was an establishment known as Dairy Farm, and on the other was a large Victorian church and rambling graveyard. Exploring the area, Nails found a decent garden shed in a corner of the graveyard, well hidden behind an overgrown yew-hedge, and he moved in there with his sleeping-bag. From the open door of the shed he had a good view of Firelight grazing and she got to know where he was and would come up to the hedge close by and wait for titbits. It wasn't bad at all, although not as convenient as the refrigerator factory. But the fattening fields way down the arterial would have been hopeless. Nails had hoped Biddy would have foregone her offer to meet him out of school the next day, or at least be late so that he would have a chance of escaping her clutches, but when he came out she was there outside the gate on her motor-bike, and there was no escaping.

'I've brought my spare helmet, so we're all legal. Get on.'

He put on the helmet and climbed on the pillion. Biddy drove out of town fast, and down narrow lanes into the country of wide marshland and wider skies which Nails knew existed but had never set eyes on before. An urban lad, such wide open spaces made him feel exposed and uncomfortable. He was suspicious of the visit anyway, not wanting to change his ways. Without Firelight, the competition held no appeal any longer.

Perhaps sensing his reluctance Biddy was stern with

him. She pulled up in a fair-sized stableyard attached to a farm which appeared to be miles from anywhere. Flat fields interspersed by dykes gleaming in the June sunshine spread as far as the eye could see and skylarks hovered and trilled overhead, but Nails, cautiously taking it all in, was given no time for comment.

'You need taking in hand, Mr Nicholson,' Biddy said sternly. She undid her helmet and shook out her frizzled hair. 'You think, just because Firelight is now out of action, that this competition is not your scene any longer. Isn't that true?'

Nails did not reply.

'And I think, after all the hours I have put in for nothing teaching you to ride, that you owe it to me to do your level best to win this competition. You *owe it to me.*' She nearly spat the words at him, her eyes holding his defiantly, making him feel very un-comfortable.

'I never said –'

'No. You don't need to say. Your lack of concern about having no horse to ride is quite apparent. The others are ten times more worried than you are. But you are going to have a horse, Nails, and you have two weeks in which to learn to ride it, and you are going to have to work damned hard, because it's a damned hard horse to ride. Do you understand me?'

Nails gaped. 'We haven't got another horse.'

'Speak for yourself. I happen to have half a dozen, and there is one, just one, that I am allowing you the privilege of riding, because I think you are capable of coping with it. Come with me.'

She put a hand on his shoulder and marched him into her tack-room at the end of the yard.

'You don't ride any horse of mine looking like a scarecrow. Put these on – I got some clothes that will fit you, and you can use for the competition. And this –'

There was a pair of cream jodhpurs and boots to go with them and a proper crash-helmet like jockeys used. Nails put them on because he had no choice, the mood Biddy was in.

'Now you'll ride my horse and we'll see how you get on. He'll feel a whole lot different from Firelight, I'm warning you.'

Nails wasn't quite sure what had hit him. Biddy's horse was sixteen hands high and a thoroughbred. It was young and inexperienced – 'like you,' she said – but, unlike him, full of spirit and raring to go. It felt like ten Firelights rolled into one.

'I know you can do it,' Biddy said unrelenting, and called for Nails after school every day on her motor-bike to subject him to another two-hour session on the aptly named Switchback. She schooled him on the lunge and in a fenced paddock over jumps, and then out in the fields and then out on the marshes, accompanying him on her own eventer and leading him over ditches and fences. Nails, getting the taste of it, stopped being terrified and began to keep his eyes open long enough to judge the thoroughbred's stride as he approached a jump and to know when he was going to stand off and when he was going to put a quick one in. He found it exhilarating – both terrifying and deeply satisfying.

Smoky

WILL JAMES

This is the ending of a classic American book, the life-story of the cow-pony Smoky. After great days, happy days, with his cowboy Clint, Smoky falls on hard times. He becomes vicious through bad treatment and achieves fame as the toughest bucking bronco in the West. They call him The Cougar. But when he gets old and clapped out he is sold to be a hireling. His new name is Cloudy. This is the classic ending for such a book, the fortunes coming full circle as in *Black Beauty*. From near-death, the deliverance . . . it is neither trite nor strained, but perfect.

★

A Many-men Horse

Fine warm spring days came, the kind of days when folks and animals alike hunt for a place where the sun shines the best. The last storm of the season had left, and as it went the last of Cloudy's rest had come to an end. That pony was rearing to go (as best as he could) when the young lady came and saddled him one bright afternoon; and as she'd been cooped up considerable herself, her spirits more than agreed with that of the horse.

Out of the stable old Cloudy went, his legs hardly feeling the stiffness that was in 'em, and seeming like his hoofs was more for flying and not at all for touching the ground. The old pony acted like he wanted to go so bad that the girl didn't have the heart to hold him back; besides the stable man had told her one time that it wouldn't hurt to let him run once in a while, if for a short ways; so, leaning ahead on her saddle, she let the horse go.

Cloudy et up the distance and brought up sudden changes of scenery as mile after mile was covered and left behind. With the warming up of the run, the stiffness went out of his legs. He felt near young again, and was taking the steep hills more like a four-year-old than the old stove up horse he was. Sweat begin a dripping from him, and as the gait was kept up, that sweat turned to white lather.

His whole hide was soaked and steaming from the

heat of his body, but he kept right on a wanting to go, and like the girl, the excitement of the run had got a holt of him till neither realized they was carrying a good thing too far. The girl's hair was flying in the breeze that was stirred. She'd lost her hat, but she wasn't caring. To be going and splitting up some more of that breeze had got to the girl's head, and cheeks flushed and a smiling she was sure getting a heap of joy out of just being alive and a going.

The trail followed along a stream and up a canyon; it kept a getting steeper and steeper, and the old horse begin to breathe harder and harder, till finally, his wide open nostrils couldn't take on enough air to do him no more. He had to slow down or else drop in his tracks, but Cloudy didn't slow down, and not a sign showed on him that he was wanting to. He was the kind of a horse that never quit and would keep right on a going till his heart stopped.

The girl, not at all realizing, kept a riding and enjoying the fast pace for all she was worth. She might of rode the old pony to his death that afternoon, only, the trail stopped and she couldn't follow it no further. It had washed out during the spring thaw, and a place ten feet wide and as deep had cut the trail in two.

She stopped there, and coming out of the trance the fast ride had put her in, she started looking for a place to cross, but there wasn't any, and the only way left was to go back on the trail she'd come.

She put her hands on Cloudy's neck like to tell

him how it was 'too bad the trail stopped short that way' but she never got to say the words. The feel of the sweat and lather that covered the horse left her dumb, and then she noticed how hard he was breathing.

The thrill of the run had turned to sudden worry and fear for what she might of done, and another sort of excitement took a holt of her as she realized and then wondered what to do. She stepped away from the horse and wide-eyed looked at him. She'd never seen a horse shake and quiver all over like that one was doing. He seemed like hardly able to stand up, rocked back and forth like he was going to keel over any minute. Cloudy was 'jiggered'★ and his staggering scared her all the more. She must do something, and quick.

The first thing that came to her was to try and cool him off before, as she figgered, he fainted from being overheated. She tore at the saddle and worked at the latigos till it was loosened, then she pulled it off and with the blanket throwed it to the ground. Steam raised off the pony's back, and at the sight of that the girl got excited all the more. Then she spotted the mountain stream below and just a little ways.

She led the horse careful and over to it, and then, thinking steady of quick ways to cool the horse off, she figgered it a good idea to lead him in the water and where it was the deepest. She skipped from boulder to boulder till finally a place was found where the

★ Overrun

water came up above the pony's knees, and there she let him stand, while with her cupped hands she splashed the cold snow water on his chest, shoulders, and back.

A half an hour or so of that, and the horse at last quit quivering, showed signs that he was cooled off and got his breath all OK again. After a while he drank, and then drank some more, and the girl watching him felt sure that the worst was over and that the horse was saved. She smiled, petted him on the neck, and felt relieved at the natural way he'd got to acting again.

The sun was hitting for the tall peaks to the west when the girl finally decided Cloudy was all right again and fit to start back. He was good and dry by then and felt cool; she'd kept him in the shade all the while, and being that mountain shade is not at all warm at that time of the year, the old pony was near shivering from the cold by the time the girl led him back to the saddle and put it on him again.

The ride back to the stable was like a funeral march as compared with the one starting out. The horse was kept on a slow walk all the way, and every care was taken by the girl so that only the easiest trail was followed. She worried as she rode along and noticed that the horse didn't seem to be the same as before; his step wasn't so sure and he'd stumble when there was nothing on the ground for him to stumble on, and then he'd sway like he was weak.

It was away after dark when finally the stable was

reached, the stable man was there and waiting, and greeting the young lady with a smile he asked:

'Did you water Cloudy before you left?'

'No,' says the girl, 'but I watered him on the mountain where I turned to come back.'

'The reason I asked, is because the new stable boy I hired forgot to water him this morning, or he thought *I* did.'

The grey-haired man didn't get to ride Cloudy the next day, nor did anybody else, for that horse was hardly able to even get out of the stall; his legs was like so many sticks of wood and with no more bend in 'em than them same sticks have. His head hung near to the ground, and not a spear of the hay that'd been put in the manger had been touched.

The girl came to the stable that noon, and would of cried at the sight of him, only the stable man came up, and she held the tears back best as she could.

'Looks like he's done for,' says that feller as he came up. He didn't ask the girl what she'd done, cause a look at the horse told him the whole story better than the girl could of; and as he figgered, a man has to take them chances when he's renting horses out that way. Besides, the girl looked so downhearted about it that he didn't have the heart to do any more but try to cheer her up.

'I'll doctor him up the best I can, and maybe get him to come out of it a little.'

The girl took hopes at them words, and her eyes a shining, asked:

'And can I come and help you?'

Every day from then on the time the girl had used a riding Cloudy was spent in the stable and by that horse. Liniments and medicines of all kinds was dug up and bought and used, and as the stable man watched her trying to do her best, he'd only shake his head. He knowed it was no use, and if the horse did come out of it, he'd never come out of it enough to ever be of any use as a saddle horse again.

The horse had been foundered. The twenty-four hours without water, the hard run and sweating up, and then cooled off sudden in ice-cold water, and drinking his fill of that same water, and all at once, had crippled him and stoved him up in a way where he'd be plum useless, only maybe for slow work and hooked to a wagon.

A month went by, and the doctoring went on, the girl always a hoping; and then one day she came to the stable to find the horse gone. She hunted up the stable man and finally, after a lot of running around, found him up in the hay loft.

'I figered,' says that feller on finding himself cornered, 'that it'd be best to turn him loose. There's good range up north a ways and thinking it'd do him more good to be loose that way on good feed, I just took him up there.'

But there was no good range in that country, not for many miles. The stable man had lied to save the girl's feelings. And instead, realizing that he couldn't turn the horse loose only maybe to let him starve, and being he couldn't afford to keep and feed a useless horse, there'd been only one way out. He'd sold him to a man who bought old horses and killed 'em for chicken feed.

Dark Clouds, Then Tall Grass

The man collecting old wore-out and crippled horses had come along and led him away. He had a little salt-grass pasture a short distance out of town, and there's where he took the old horse. He turned him loose amongst a few more old horses, and would keep him there till the time come when some 'chicken man' around town would need the carcass of one of the horses to feed to his chickens; then the horse what looked like it had the shortest to live would be killed and hauled away.

It didn't look like the end was very far for the mouse-coloured horse. All the work he'd done and the interest he'd had while under the names of Smoky and The Cougar, had stopped being accounted for, and sort of pinched out under the name of Cloudy; and now he had no name. He was just 'chicken feed', and soon, if he stayed in that pasture, all what he'd been and done would be blotted out with the crack of a rifle shot.

But the old pony had no hint of that, and as it was he wasn't for quitting as yet. His old stiff legs was still able to carry him around some, the doctoring he'd got at the stable had helped him more than what had been hoped, and then getting out in a pasture where he could keep moving around as he wanted to was helping him some more. Besides, his old heart was still strong, quite a bit solid meat was covering his ribs, and with the salt and wire grass to graze on he could still make out and mighty well.

A few weeks went by when once in a while and every few days, one of the old horses he was pasturing with was caught, led out, a rifle shot was heard, and he'd never be seen no more. Other old horses was brought in and they'd pasture on with him till one by one they'd also disappear only to be replaced by more of 'em.

The old mouse-coloured horse must of looked like he was good to live for a long time yet; anyway, the 'chicken horse' man had kept him, maybe for emergency, and so he wouldn't be out of horses if an order for one came; and that kind was hard to get.

Then one day, a man came, looked all the old horses over. And finally, like he'd decided, pointed a finger towards the horse that'd last been known as Cloudy. That pony was caught and led out the same way other horses had disappeared, but no rifle shot was heard. Instead, a lot of parleying went on.

Cloudy was led alongside of an old bony something that'd once been a horse. The old rack of bones was hooked on to a light wagon and seeming like hardly able to stand as the eyes of the two men went from him to Cloudy, to sort of figger out which of the two was worth the most, and *how much* the most.

Finally the dickering came to an end and seemed like agreeable to both parties. Three dollars to boot was handed, and the trade was made. The rack of bones was unhooked, the harness pulled off of him, and turned loose in the chicken horse pasture. Then Cloudy's old heart missed a few beats as that same harness was picked up again and throwed over his own back.

As true a saddle horse, and once hard to set on, as the mouse-coloured horse had been, the feel of that harness on his back was as much the same as if a shovel or a hayfork had been handed to a cowpuncher with the idea of his using 'em. The old horse felt it a plain disgrace, and snorted as it was buckled around him to stay; but the black-whiskered hombre that buckled it on never seemed to notice or care that the horse had no liking for the collar and all the straps.

He kept on a fastening the harness, and when that was done, he jerked the old pony around and backed him into the shafts of the same old wagon that the rack of bones had been unhooked out of. Cloudy kept on a snorting and looked on one side and then the other as the shafts of the wagon was raised. If only he could act the way his heart wanted him to; but he didn't have the strength, the action to put in it, nor the energy no more. The most he could do was to snort, quiver, and shake his head.

But, as he was all hooked up and the man jumping in the wagon grabbed his whip, Old Cloudy done his best to try and get back to some of the life and tearing ability that'd once been his. He kicked a couple of times at the rattling thing on wheels and which he was fastened to, then he tried to buck some and finally wound up by wanting to run away; but the harness held and the rattling thing behind came right along wherever he went, and worse yet, he felt the stinging lash of the man's whip as he fought on and tried to clear himself. Then the jerking of the bit thru his mouth, and with all that to show how useless his fighting and wanting to get away really was, the old pony soon lost heart. He finally settled down to a choppy lope, then a trot that was just as choppy, and at last to a walk.

Another sting of the whip was felt on his flank, and at the same time, the line was jerked at the bit, and Cloudy, still pulling the wagon, was made to turn up a lane. At the end of the lane was a shack made of old pieces of boards and covered over with the tin of old oil-cans. To the right of that and a little ways further was another shack that looked like a mate to the first, only worse, and that one was going to be Cloudy's place of rest and shelter whenever work was over.

There he was pulled to a stop, unhooked, led to the manger, and tied. The stable door was closed with a bang, and after a while the old horse, still wanting to cling to life regardless of what came, stuck his nose in the manger to nibble on some of what was in it. He reached for a mouthful of what he'd naturally took for hay, and chewed for a spell, but he didn't chew on it long. There was a musty taste about the long dirty brown stems that didn't at all fit in with any hay he'd ever et. The kind that'd been put in the manger for him to eat was the same that the livery stableman had used to put in the stalls and bed the horses down with. It was straw, only this was musty straw and wouldn't even make good bedding for horses.

Cloudy felt hungry long before the next morning came, and often thru the night he'd nosed into the musty straw with the hopes of finding a few stems that'd do to fill an empty space, but there wasn't any to be found. The old rack of bones that'd been there before him had looked for some too, and with no better luck. Cloudy's new owner figgered it cheaper to swap horses with the 'chicken man' and give him a few dollars to boot whenever any horse of his give out; he wasn't going to buy no high-priced hay for no horse. The straw was given to him for the getting and would keep any horse alive and working for at least six months, and then, or whenever the horse would be too weak to go any more, he'd trade him for another. Any kind of a horse, fat or thin, could always be used by the chicken man, and in trade, he'd always take one of the fattest to take the place of the one he'd just starved near to death. That way, year in year out, he'd keep a draining the last of the life of every horse he'd get his claws on to.

His property, and where he starved the horses into making a living for him, took in a couple of acres. Half of that land was rocks, mostly, and where he kept a few chickens. He bought, or stole a little grain for *them*; but they well repaid him. Every time he went to town there was a basket of eggs in his wagon and which he sold well. The other half of this land was cultivated, and where vegetables of all kinds had been made to grow. There's where the help of a horse was needed, to pull the cultivator or the plough, then the hauling of the vegetables to town, and once there, any odd job that could be got and which would bring a few dollars for the use of the horse and wagon.

It was bright and early the next morning when the work begin for Cloudy. The man showed his teeth in a grin as he looked in the manger while putting the harness on the horse, and noticing the straw in there hadn't hardly been touched, remarked:

'You'll be eating some of that before you get thru.'

Cloudy was made acquainted with many different kinds of implements and work that day. All was mighty strange and plum against the ways of working which he'd been broke to do. It was pull, and pull, one contraption and then another, back and forth thru furrows, turn at the end and then back again. If he slowed down, or hesitated, wondering what to do, there was the whip always on hand to make him decide and mighty quick.

As the long days run into weeks and the work in

the field and in the town got to bearing down on him, the old pony even got so he couldn't hate no more; abuse or kindness had both got to be the same, and one brought out no more results or show of interest than the other. He went to the jerk of the lines like without realizing; and when he was finally led into the stable when night come the feeling was the same. There he et the musty straw because it was under his nose. He didn't mind the taste of it, he didn't mind anything, any more.

Of the odd jobs that Cloudy's owner would get to do around town and whenever he could get away from his truck and chicken farm, there was one which he looked forward to the most, and which the thought of made him rub his hands together with pleasure. It was that of scattering the posters advertising The Annual Rodeo, and Celebration, that was pulled off in town and every early fall. But that wasn't all. There was many other things for him to do at that time for which he could charge without anybody ever finding out whether all he'd been paid to do really had been done.

That year as usual he was ready, and right on the dot, to take on some more of that kind of work. He'd hooked up the old mouse-coloured horse and taking a load of vegetables on the way in, stuck around town doing the different kinds of work the rodeo association had furnished him with. He'd be on the go all day and prodding the old horse into a trot, sometimes even if the wagon was loaded.

It'd be away into the night before he'd turn the tired horse towards home. Every day was a great day, *for the man*, there was so many people around to make the town lively; and being most of 'em was strangers, he could get to within talking distance of 'em easy enough, and a few would even stand to have him around for a few minutes at the time.

Them strangers had come to see the rodeo. Most of 'em was from other towns around, and mixed in the crowd once in a while could be seen the high-crowned hat of a cowboy who'd come to ride, rope, and bulldog. Then at the Casa Grande Hotel, and registered there, was many cattle buyers from the northern States.

Two of the buyers was setting in the lobby of the hotel one morning and a talking on the first day's event of the rodeo. A telegraph pole stuck up right before their vision and on the edge of the sidewalk, and nailed to that pole was a poster advertising the rodeo, and with a photograph of a bucking horse in action on it, told all about 'the great bucking horse and outlaw The Grey Cougar, the only one that could compare, in wickedness and bucking ability, to The Cougar, that once famous man killing horse.'

The two went on to talking about the rodeo, and naturally the talk drifted on about The Grey Cougar, and '*how* he could buck'.

'The boys tell me,' says one of the men, 'that this Grey Cougar horse couldn't hold a candle to the real Cougar when it come to bucking and fighting.

According to that, the other horse must of been *some* wicked.'

The man was still talking on the subject, when an old mouse-coloured house, pulling an old wagon loaded down with vegetables, came to a stiff-legged stop, and right by the telegraph pole on which the poster telling all about The Grey Cougar was nailed. The man in the lobby grinned a little at the sight of the old horse a standing there like in comparison with the famous grey outlaw, and pointing a finger in his direction, he remarked:

'There must be the Old Cougar right there, Clint. Anyway he's got the same colour.'

The man called Clint grinned some at the joke, but the grin soon faded away as he kept a looking at the old horse, and noticed the condition he was in. Then he seen the saddle-marks that was all over the pony's back, and he says:

'You can never tell, that old pony might of been mighty hard to set at one time too – but the way he looks like now, them times are sure done past and gone.'

'Yep,' agreed the other man, 'it's a miracle that pony can navigate at all – I wonder how it is that this Humane Society hombre that's sticking around the rodeo grounds don't happen to notice such as this. I'd like to help hang a feller for driving a horse like that around.'

The conversation was held up for a spell as the two men watched the bewhiskered man come out of the hotel with an empty basket and climbed the wagon on which the old mouse-coloured horse was hooked. He grabbed the lines and the whip both at the same time and went to work a putting the horse into a trot.

Clint was for getting up as he seen the whip land on the old pony's hide, but the other man grabbed a hold of his arm and says:

'Never mind, old boy, most likely that Humane Society outfit'll fall on the bolshevik's neck before he gets very far.'

The man called Clint set down again, but he was boiling up inside, and he didn't at all look pleasant as the conversation was resumed and noticed how his friend turned it to other things and away from the subject of old horses and such.

The last day of the rodeo had come, and Clint was to start with his train-load of stock that night. Him and his friend was setting in the lobby of the hotel that evening a talking and wondering when they'd be seeing one another again, when outside and by the telegraph pole, came the same old mouse-coloured horse and stopped not an inch from where the two men had seen him a couple of days before.

Both was quick to spot him again this time, and right then, for some reason or other, the conversation died down. The first sight of that old pony hadn't been forgot, and when he showed up this second time, right before their eyes, he was like reminding 'em, and natural like, set the two men to thinking. That old shadow of a horse told some of the hard knocks of life, of things that was past and gone and which could of been bettered while the bettering could be done.

It was while the thinking was going on that way, that Clint sort of felt a faint, far-away something a knocking and from down the bottom of his think tank. That something was trying hard to come back to life as that man's eyes kept a going over the pony's blazed face and bony frame, but it was buried so far underneath so many things that'd been stacked there that the knocking was pretty well muffled up. It'd have to be helped by some sort of a sudden jolt before it could come out on top.

The jolt came as the vegetable man got his seat on the wagon and as usual reached for the whip. Clint's friend a trying to keep him from running out and starting a rompus had tried to draw his interest by asking:

'What's become of that cowhorse *Smoky*, that used to –?'

But the question was left for *him* to wonder about, for Clint wasn't there to answer. Instead the hotel door slammed and only a glimpse of that same cowboy could be seen as he passed by the lobby window. In less than it takes to tell it, he was up on the wagon, took a bulldogging holt of the surprised vegetable man, and by his whiskers, dragged him off his seat and down to earth.

The telephone on the desk of the sheriff's office

rang till it near danced a jig, and when that feller lifted the receiver, a female voice was heard to holler: 'Somebody is killing somebody else with a whip, by the Casa Grande Hotel. *Hurry! Quick!*'

The sheriff appeared on the scene and took in the goings on at a glance. Like a man who knowed his business, his eyes went to looking for what might of caused the argument as he came. He looked at the old horse whose frame showed thru the hide, then the whip marks on that hide. He knowed horses as well as he did men; and when he noticed more marks of the same whip on the bewhiskered man's face, he stood his ground, watched, and then grinned.

'Say, cowboy,' he finally says, 'don't scatter that hombre's remains too much; you know we got to keep record and I don't want to be looking all over the streets to find out who he *was*.'

Clint turned at the sound of the voice, and sizing up the grinning sheriff, went back to his victim and broke the butt end of the whip over his head; after which he wiped his hands, and proceeded to unhook the old horse off the wagon.

That evening was spent in 'investigating'. Clint and the sheriff went to the chicken-horse man and found out enough from him about the vegetable man and his way of treating horses to put that hombre in a cool place and keep him there for a spell.

'I'm glad to've caught on to that feller's doings,' remarks the sheriff as him and Clint went to the livery stable, their next place of investigation.

There Clint listened mighty close as he learned a heap about the mouse-coloured horse when he was known as Cloudy. The stable man went on to tell as far as he knowed about the horse and the whole history of him, and when that pony was known thru the Southwest and many other places, as *The Cougar*, the wickedest bucking horse and fighting outlaw the country had ever layed eyes on.

Clint was kinda proud in hearing that. He'd heard of The Cougar and that pony's bucking ability even up to the Canadian line and across it, and to himself he says: 'That Smoky horse never did do things half-ways.' But he got to wondering, and then asked how come the pony had turned out to be that kind of a horse. That, the stable man didn't know. It was news to him that the horse had ever been anything else, and as he says:

'The first that was seen of that horse is when some cowboys found him on the desert, amongst a bunch of wild horses, and packing a saddle. Nobody had ever showed up to claim him, and as that pony had been more than inclined to buck and fight is how come he was sold as a bucking horse – and believe me, old timer,' went on the stable man, a shaking his head, 'he was *some* bucking horse.'

'Well,' says the sheriff, 'that's another clue run to the ground with nothing left of, but the remains.'

That night, the big engine was hooked on to the trainload of cattle as to per schedule and started puffing its way on to the north. In the last car, the one next to the caboose, and the least crowded, a space had been partitioned off. In that space was a bale of good hay, a barrel of water, and an old mouse-coloured horse.

The winter that came was very different to any the old mouse-coloured horse had ever put in. The first part of it went by with him like in a trance, not realizing and hardly seeing. His old heart had dwindled down till only a sputtering flame was left, and that threatened to go out with the first hint of any kind of breeze.

Clint had got the old horse in a warm box-stall, filled the manger full of the best blue joint hay there was, and even bedded him down with more of the same; water was in that same stall and where it could be easy reached, and then that cowboy had bought many a dollar's worth of condition powders, and other preparations which would near coax life back even in a dead body.

Two months went by when all seemed kinda hopeless, but Clint worked on and kept a hoping. He'd brought the old horse in the house, and made him a bed by the stove if that would of helped; and far as that goes, he'd of done anything else, just so a spark of life showed in the old pony's eyes; but he'd done all he could do, and as he'd lay a hand on the old skinny neck and felt of the old hide, he'd cuss and wish for the chance of twisting out of shape who all had been responsible. Then his expression would change, and he'd near bust out crying as he'd think back and compare the old wreck with what that horse had been.

As much as Clint had liked Smoky, the old wreck of a shadow of that horse wasn't wanting for any of the same liking. It was still in the cowboy's heart a plenty, and if anything, more so on account that the old pony was now needing help, and a friend like he'd never needed before; and Clint was more on hand with the horse, now that he was worthless, than he'd been when Smoky was the four hundred dollar cow-horse and worth more.

Finally, and after many a day of care and worrying, Clint begin to notice with a glad smile that the pony's hide was loosening up. Then after a week or so more of showing hay and grain, condition powers, and other things down the old pony's throat, a layer of meat begin to spread over them bones and under that hide. Then one day a spark showed in the pony's eyes, soon after that he started taking interest in the things around.

As layer after layer of meat and then tallow accumulated and rounded the sharp corners of Smoky's frame, that pony was for noticing more and more till after a while his interest spread enough, and with a clearer vision, went as far as to take in the man, who kept a going and coming, once in a while touched him, and then talked.

Clint liked to had a fit one day, when talking to the horse and happened to say *Smoky*, he noticed that pony cock an ear.

The recuperating of the horse went pretty fast from then on; and as the winter days howled past and early spring drawed near, there was no more fear of Smoky's last stand being anywheres near. As the days growed longer and the sun got warmer, there was times when Clint would lead the horse out and turn him loose to walk around in the sunshine, and that way get the blood to circulating. Smoky would sometimes mosey along for hours around the place and then start out on some trail, but always when the sun went down, he was by the stable door again and then Clint would let him in.

Clint would watch him by the hour whenever the horse was out that way, and he'd wonder, as he kept his eye on him, if that pony remembered, if the knocks he'd got from different people in different countries, didn't forever make him forget his home range and all that went with it. Not many miles away was where he was born; the big mountains now covered with snow was the same he was raised on, and which he tore up with his hoofs as he played while a little colt, and by his mammy. The corrals by the stable and sheds was the ones he was first run into when branded, and in them, a few years later, broke to saddle; but what Clint would wonder the most, as he watched, is whether Smoky remembered *him*.

The cowboy had kept a hoping that sometime he'd be greeted with a nicker as he'd open the stable door in the morning. Clint felt if the horse remembered, he would nicker that way at the sight of him and like he used to; but morning after morning went by, and even tho Smoky seemed full of life and rounded out to near natural again, no nicker was ever heard.

'Somebody must of stretched that pony's heartstrings to the breaking point,' he remarked one day, as he'd stopped, wondering as usual, and looked at the horse.

Finally spring came sure enough, and broke up the winter. Green grass-covered ridges took the place of snow banks, and the cottonwoods along the creeks was beginning to bud. It was during one of them fine spring days, when riding along and looking the country over, Clint run acrost a bunch of horses. In the bunch was a couple of colts just a few days old, and knowing that old ponies have such a strong interest and liking for the little fellers, the cowboy figgered the sight of 'em would help considerable in bringing Smoky's heart up a few notches, and maybe to remembering. He fell in behind the bunch and hazed 'em all towards the corrals, and as Smoky, turned loose that day, spotted the bunch, his head went up. Then he noticed the little fellers, and that old pony, gathering all the speed there was in him, headed straight for the bunch and amongst 'em.

Clint corralled him and all the rest together and setting on his horse at the gate, watched Smoky while that horse was having the time of his life getting acquainted. The pony dodged kicks and bites and went back and forth thru the bunch, and a spark showed in his eye which hadn't been there for many a day.

The cowboy could near see the horse smile at the little colts; and he was surprised at the show of action and interest the old pony had reserved, or gained. He was acting near like a two-year-old, and Clint grinned as he watched.

'Daggone his old hide,' says the cowboy, 'it looks to me like he's good to live and enjoy life for many summers yet'; then thinking strong, he went on, 'and maybe in that time he might get to remembering me again – I wonder.'

He watched Smoky a while longer and till he got acquainted some, and at last deciding it'd be for the best to let him go, he reined his horse out of the gate and let the bunch run by. The old pony seemed to hesitate some as the bunch filed out. He liked their company mighty well but something held him back; then a horse nickered, and even tho that nicker might not of been meant for him, it was enough to make him decide. He struck out on a high lope and towards the bunch. One of the little colts and full of play waited for him, and nipping the old horse in the flanks, run by his side till the bunch was caught up with – Smoky was *living* again.

Clint sat on his horse and watched the bunch lope out over a ridge and out of sight; and with a last glimpse at the mouse-coloured rump he grinned a little, but it was a sorry grin, and as he kept a looking the way Smoky had gone, he says:

'I wonder if he ever will.'

★

With the green grass growing near an inch a day, Clint wasn't worried much on how old Smoky was making it. He figgered a horse couldn't die if he wanted to, not on that range at that time of the year; but some day soon he was going to try and locate the old horse and find out for sure how he really was. Then a lot of work came on which kept the cowboy from going out soon as he wanted to, and then one morning, bright and early, as he stepped out to get a bucket of water, the morning sun throwed a shadow on the door; and as he stuck his head out a nicker was heard.

Clint dropped his bucket in surprise at what he heard and then seen. For, standing out a ways, slick and shiny, was the old mouse-coloured horse. The good care the cowboy had handed him, and afterwards, the ramblings over the old home range, had done its work. The heart of Smoky had come to life again, and full size.

Acknowledgements

The editor and publishers gratefully acknowledge the following for permission to reproduce copyright material in this book.

'National Velvet' by Enid Bagnold from *National Velvet*, published by William Heinemann Ltd, copyright © author's estate, 1935, reprinted by permission of the publisher; 'A Pony for Jean' by Joanna Cannan from *A Pony for Jean*, published by The Bodley Head, copyright © the estate of Joanna Cannan, 1936, reprinted by permission of the executors of the Joanna Cannan Estate; 'Another Pony for Jean' by Joanna Cannan from *Another Pony for Jean*, published by Collins, copyright © the estate of Joanna Cannan, reprinted by permission of the executors of the Joanna Cannan Estate; 'The Black Brigade' by W. J. Gordon from *The Horse World of London*, published by J. A. Allen in conjuction with David & Charles, copyright

© J. A. Allen & Co Ltd, 1971, reprinted by permission of J. A. Allen & Co Ltd; 'Smoky' by Will James from *Smoky the Cow Horse*, published by Charles Scribner's Sons, copyright © Charles Scribner's Sons, 1926, reprinted by permission of the publisher; 'Who, Sir? Me, Sir?' by K. M. Peyton from *Who, Sir? Me, Sir?*, published by Oxford University Press, copyright © K. M. Peyton, 1983, reprinted by permission of the publisher; 'Horse of Air' by Lucy Rees from *Horse of Air*, published by Faber & Faber Ltd, copyright © Faber & Faber Ltd, 1980, reprinted by permission of the publisher; 'Jump for Joy' by Pat Smythe from *Jump for Joy*, published by Cassell & Co Ltd, copyright © Pat Smythe, 1954, reprinted by permission of the author.

Every effort has been made to trace copyright holders, but in a few cases this has proved impossible. The editor and publishers apologize for these cases of unwilling copyright transgression and would like to hear from any copyright holders not acknowledged.